MW01287511

HARD CONTACT

A BREED THRILLER

CAMERON CURTIS

INKUBATOR
BOOKS

Published by Inkubator Books
www.inkubatorbooks.com

ISBN (eBook): 978-1-83756-332-6
ISBN (Paperback): 978-1-83756-333-3

Για την Ολυμπία

Northern
Sporades   Skiros
Euboea
Chalcis

☐ATHENS
Piraeus

Lesbos   Mitilini

Chios

South Greece
Gateway to the
Aegean

Andros
Tinos   Icaria
Ermoupoli   Mykonos
Cyclades
Paros   Naxos

Samos

Amorgos   Kos

Milos

Santorini   Dodecanese

Rhodes
Rhodes

Karpathos

Chania
Heraklion
Rethymno   Crete

Gavdos

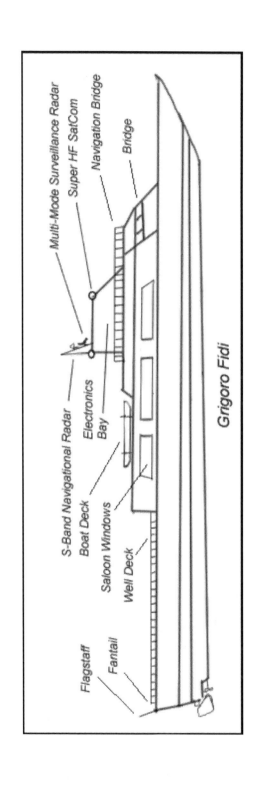

Multi-Mode Surveillance Radar

Super HF SatCom

Navigation Bridge

Bridge

S-Band Navigational Radar

Electronics Bay

Boat Deck

Saloon Windows

Well Deck

Flagstaff

Fantail

Grigoro Fidi

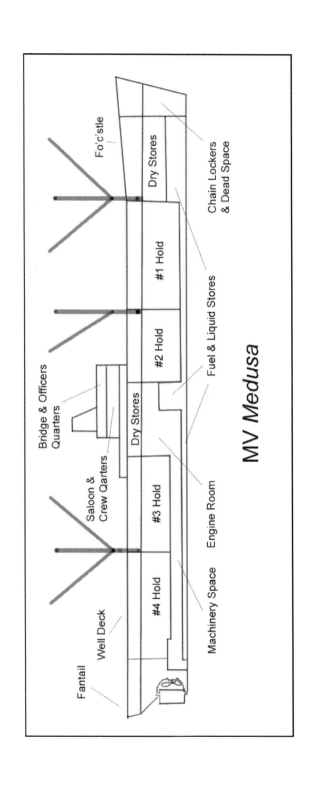

MV *Medusa*

MH-60 Sea Hawk

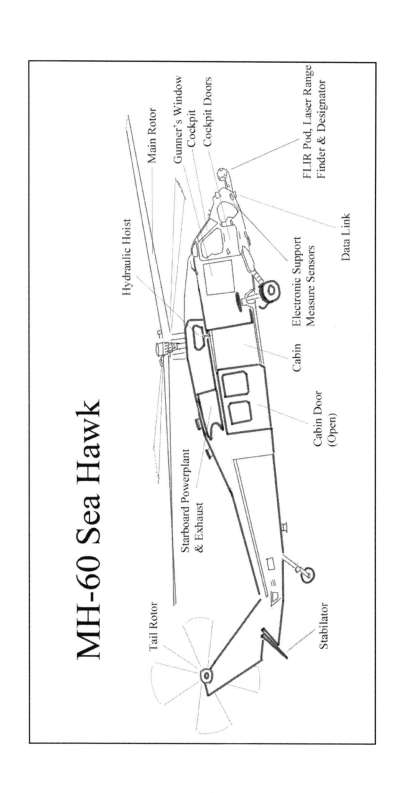

Tail Rotor

Starboard Powerplant & Exhaust

Hydraulic Hoist

Main Rotor

Gunner's Window

Cockpit

Cockpit Doors

FLIR Pod, Laser Range Finder & Designator

Data Link

Electronic Support Measure Sensors

Cabin

Cabin Door (Open)

Stabilator

1

THE FIRST DAY – EVENING, THE GOLIATH

G*oliath*. My palm is flat on the bottom half of the G. The paint is peeling from the rusty metal surface of the ship's fantail. This rust bucket hasn't been painted in years. Certainly not in the last forty-eight hours.

I withdraw my hand, cling to the climbing rope. My feet, shod in slip-resistant water moccasins, are locked in. My weight rests on one of the knots tied every three feet, to provide hand and footholds. The top end of the rope is attached to a rubber-covered hook. Thrown over a rail, jammed hard against a stanchion. Tension is provided by my weight. My aqualung, weight belt and swim fins hang fastened at the bottom of the rope. They lie under the surface of the water, where they are easy to recover.

Boarding doesn't get much easier than this. A routine "hook and climb"—sea state one, rippled calm, a stationary vessel. When the target ship is underway—sea state five, nine-foot waves—things get sporty.

Stein and I found the *Goliath*'s transponder signals anomalous. At any other time, the anomalies might have been innocent. But we're looking for a missing vessel loaded with two billion dollars worth of gold. We can't afford to ignore anything.

Dressed in a black neoprene wetsuit, I blend into the shadows. Water drips from the diving mask perched on the crown of my head. I hold my breath, listen for the sound of footsteps on the deck above. Nothing.

The *Goliath* is a small freighter of six thousand tons. A ship this size should have a crew of between twelve and fifteen men. It's the middle of the evening, and the crew is probably in the saloon. The ship is safe in Port Cymos, on the northwest coast of Rhodes. There should be two men on watch. One on the bridge, another in the engine room.

I scan the poop deck, then the well deck. Two lifeboats hang from their davits, one on either side of the ship. There are paint lockers and funnels. Along the center line are cargo hatches three and four. Portholes in the superstructure glow with orange light and cast the decks into deep shadow.

A waterproof bag is slung at my waist. Inside are a Heckler & Koch Mark 23 pistol, a hooded flashlight, and a waterproof survival radio. I hold the Mark 23 in my right hand, the flashlight in my left. The Mark 23 is decocked, with a round in the chamber. The flashlight is off. My thumb rests lightly on the switch.

The best way to get access to the holds is through the superstructure. There are exterior companionways on either side that lead to the saloon. They switch back and take you to the wings of the bridge deck.

I step forward, cross the poop, and descend a companionway to the well deck. Walk to an oval watertight door that has been propped open. I stop at the vestibule, strain my senses for any sign of a threat. Hold the Mark 23 low at my leg.

Inside, my eyes adjust to the gloom. Tables and chairs are bolted to the deck. Cabinets have been bolted to bulkheads. To allow air to circulate, the portholes stand open. An interior companionway leads upstairs to the saloon. The tinny sound of Greek voices issues from a cheap television.

Portside, a second interior companionway leads into the bowels of the ship. I walk to it, catch my left shoulder on a half-open cabinet door. Pain shoots through my arm.

The cabinet door has swung open to reveal an arsenal. I slip the Mark 23 back into its plastic case, cover the flashlight with the palm of my hand, and flick it on. The flesh between my fingers glows red. I point the flashlight into the cabinet and allow a bit of light to shine through.

These people are keeping Heckler & Koch in business. The sailors on this ship like G3 battle rifles, USP pistols, and MP5 submachine guns. The G3 is a NATO 7.62mm/.308 caliber rifle good for long work. The MP5s and USPs are good for close quarters. The 9mm round is small for my taste. It will stop average bad guys, rodents, and annoying in-laws. Never shoot a heavy-caliber man with a small-caliber bullet.

I count half a dozen G3s and as many MP5s. The USPs lie on a shelf. USP 9mm pistols are hard to distinguish from Bundeswehr P8s. I pick one up and examine its safety lever. USP safeties thumb-down to fire, military P8s thumb-up. These pistols are commercial USPs, not military.

There's a big box on the floor of the cabinet. Simple, planed wood. Lot numbers stenciled on the side, rope handles on either end. I lift the lid. Inside is a wooden tray of

fifteen M67 fragmentation grenades. The box is deep enough
for two trays, thirty grenades in total.

Goliath is a pirate ship. With this much lethal hardware,
its crew must be a cutthroat bunch.

I hood the flashlight and descend the companionway
into the hold. The ship is a tin can. Companionway steps are
steel grates and bulkheads are rust-covered metal. To allow
air to circulate, the watertight doors have been propped
open. If the ship is holed in this condition, it will flood and
sink without a trace.

All four holds stand empty. The air smells of rusty water.
I cast the light around, examine vast brown curtains of
corrosion that bleed from the overhead and pour in sheets
over the bulkheads. Puddles on the steel floor ripple. A
single engine is kept running to supply the ship's electricity.

Goliath carries no cargo.

Outside, I ascend the starboard companionway, look
through the saloon's lighted portholes. Men are watching
television and playing cards.

I climb to the bridge. Three stories above the well deck,
the vast sweep of Port Cymos's commercial port spreads
before me. Three hundred yards to my left, a long spit of
land separates the commercial harbor from the recreational.
That spit is where I concealed my Zodiac. On the other side,
Stein is waiting at the Golden Paradise Hotel. It overlooks
the bay from the top of a three-hundred-foot cliff.

There must be a man on the bridge. I strain my ears,
listen to the whisper of waves against the sides of the ship.
I'm on the starboard wing. The interior of the bridge is dark,
except for a dim glow from the radio and navigation
compartments.

The faint odor of cigarette smoke drifts in the air. The

bridge is empty, but a dark figure stands on the port wing.
He's leaning against the combing. The cherry of his cigarette
glows.

I don't have a suppressor, so I slip the Mark 23 and flashlight into the plastic bag. Draw my knife, a double-edged
Cold Steel OSS. I open the door to the bridge and cross to
the port wing. The man's back is to me. He's a burly guy, with
broad shoulders and thick biceps. Outweighs me by thirty
pounds. A 9mm USP has been stuffed in his right hip
pocket.

Step behind him, clamp my left hand over his nose and
mouth. Stab him in the neck. The point goes in the right
side and out the left. I punch the knife forward. Rip everything—esophagus, trachea, carotid arteries, jugular veins—
out the front. He gurgles beneath my hand. Black fountains
spray the combing. In seconds, his brain dies from lack of
oxygen.

The man sags. I drag him into the bridge and lay him in a
corner. Wipe my hands and blade on his jacket, slide the
knife back into its sheath.

The radio compartment beckons. I hood the flashlight
and examine the room. The ship sports three modern radios,
covering the entire transmission spectrum.

My survival radio operates in either cellular or satellite
mode. Laminated with plastic, waterproof to three hundred
feet, remote charging. In all other respects, indistinguishable
from a mobile phone. I photograph the electronic equipment. The sensor is so sensitive I can shoot in the dark
without flash.

In the navigation compartment, I photograph the GPS
equipment and AIS transponders. Ships and airplanes
transmit signals that show their location. The signals

contain the name of the vessel, its location, course, and speed.

There are two of everything. With deliberation, I photograph each device and the settings on the dials. A laptop sits in one corner of the transponder desk. The *Goliath*'s digital log. The laptop is too big to fit in my waterproof bag. There's a micro-SD reader with a one terabyte card. I pop the card and drop it in the bag. I don't know if the laptop has an internal hard drive. I draw my knife. Slide the blade between the upper and lower halves of the assembly and pry them apart. I tear off the keyboard, expose the motherboard. There's no hard drive.

The dismembered laptop lies on the desk like a gutted roach. I open the manual log, photograph the last week's entries. Replace the survival radio in the waterproof bag with the Mark 23 and seal it.

Time to go. I step back onto the bridge. I'll go down the companionway on the port wing, make my way aft, descend the rope, and exfil.

"Panayotis?"

A hulking black shape steps onto the starboard wing. He ascended the starboard companionway, just as I did. Sees me through the glass of the bridge windows, thinks I'm the bridge watch.

I can't see his face. Only a big form silhouetted against the lights of Port Cymos. He's pushing his way onto the bridge—

—reaching for a gun.

I dive through the door onto the port wing. There's the crack of a gunshot and sparks fly off the deck. I swing onto the companionway, grip the handrails with my hands and feet, slide down.

"Niko!" the man behind me shouts. "Christos! Port side!"

There's no point in having a gun battle. He's got at least half a dozen men in the saloon, with automatic weapons. I pull my mask down over my eyes and nose. He fires again, but I'm still a black wraith in my wetsuit. The bullet skids off metal.

I go to the rail, grab the mask with both hands, and jump into the harbor feet first. There's a smash as I hit the water. Streamlined, I still have to fight to keep the impact from ripping the mask from my face.

Turn, swim underwater toward the stern. Pop to the surface, fill my lungs.

"There!"

The sheer metal wall of the *Goliath*'s side towers over me. High up, muzzle flashes twinkle like fireflies. Two weapons, with extremely high rates of fire. MP5s. The way these guys fire them, MP5s are grossly inaccurate. They're pumping out lead at a prodigious rate. A hit is a hit, whether aimed or dumb luck. A moving target, I thrash the water.

"Vasilios! Bring the grenades!"

Swearing, Niko and Christos change out their mags. Another figure runs to the rail—Vasilios.

The pirates dump two more mags on me. I fill my lungs and dive. Kick as hard as I can, try to go deep. There's a thump. A terrific concussion boxes my ears and squeezes my chest. It's like blowing up a plastic bag, knotting it, and bursting it with both hands. The pressure almost forces the breath from my body.

Struggle to hold my breath, dive under the hull. Thank goodness the *Goliath* is empty and its draft is shallow.

More explosions. They're depth-charging me with grenades. The concussions are more distant, but they still shake me. They used to torture sailors this way in the nine-teenth century. It was called keel-hauling. I swim hard, praying the pirates don't guess what I'm doing.

Their leader is no fool. He's got men on both sides of the ship, and they're waiting for me starboard.

"Here! He's here!"

More automatic weapons fire. I gasp for breath, dive, and swim for the bow. Pop to the surface, draw more fire, fill my lungs.

The lunge for the bow was a feint. I turn and swim underwater for the stern. If I can get to my aqualung, I'll have a fighting chance. If they get to the stern before I do, will they spot the hook and rope? All they have to do is throw the hook into the harbor. The tank and will sink to the bottom and I'll never find it.

I try not to think. Thrash as hard as I can toward the stern. Follow the side of the ship. When it starts to curve, I know I'm almost there. Ahead—the great shadow of the rudder. Inboard of the rudder, the *Goliath*'s great screw.

There, dangling next to the rudder—my aqualung, regu-lator, and scuba gear. I grab the bottle by the neck, take the rubber mouthpiece between my teeth, turn the valve. Spit foul water, exhale, and suck blessed air. I struggle into my tank's harness, grab my weight belt and fins. Without both-ering to put them on, I dive as deep as I can. The bottom might be thirty feet deep.

Another explosion. The aqualung is life, but a closed-circuit rebreather would be better. They'll look for my bubble track. No bubbles, no troubles, and I am leaving a lot of bubbles.

I roll on my back and look up. The moon hasn't risen, and the sky above the water is black. There, dancing on the surface, I see lights. There are spotlights mounted on the superstructure and the pirates are using them to hunt for my bubble trail.

The odds are rising in my favor. Unless they lower a whaleboat and conduct a thorough search, it's unlikely they'll find my bubble track. Less likely they'll keep it, once acquired.

I sit on the bottom, don my weight belt, take off my water moccasins, and put on my flippers. The harbor bottom is littered with crap. I feel the jagged edge of a broken bottle next to my elbow. The water isn't particularly cold, but I wore a full black wetsuit for camouflage, and to protect myself from random garbage. I fasten the moccasins to my belt and consult the luminous dial of the compass strapped to my wrist. The Zodiac is waiting for me on the spit that separates us from the recreational port. It's several hundred yards due east.

First, I swim in the direction of the harbor mouth. That's to throw off my pursuers should they identify my bubble trail. After two hundred yards, I stop and look back. The lights of my pursuers are far away, close to the *Goliath*. They must have found my rope and hook by now. They know I have an aqualung. How will they react?

I'm not about to swim to Turkiye. I reorient myself and kick toward the spit where I hid the Zodiac.

Mission accomplished.

2

THE FIRST DAY – LATE EVENING, PORT CYMOS

Two miles west of Port Cymos, the Golden Paradise Hotel overlooks the Aegean from the top of a high cliff. An exclusive resort, it caters to the wealthy and pampered. It's the only kind of hotel for Anya Stein, Deputy Director of the CIA, and granddaughter of the man who gave the Stein Center to Harvard. I help her do little things like sneak onto pirate ships. The kind crewed by nasty cutthroats armed with automatic rifles, submachine guns, and hand grenades. That's what I do best, and the skill rates me worthy of a suite at her kind of hotel.

The two-hundred-yard sweep of beach is deserted. The boat and diving rental shops are shut. The moon has risen, and its cold light glints off the cliffside elevator. The glass and steel cage runs inside an iron gantry secured to the cliff face by six-foot iron spikes. The cage hangs at the top of the gantry, where its doors open to the flat lawn outside the hotel. That makes sense—the last person to leave the beach would have left the elevator at the top. When I made my way to the beach earlier in the evening, I took the winding stone stairs. I didn't want anyone in the hotel to wonder why the elevator was in operation long after everyone had left the beach.

It's not quite eleven, and the hotel lights look inviting. I sling my flippers over my shoulder and put on my moccasins. Haul the Zodiac from the surf and onto the beach. Carry my gear to the rental shack.

The shack's as I left it hours ago. I'd forced the lock and borrowed the aqualung, weights and fins I needed. I wore my own wetsuit, carried the waterproof bag with my weapon, flashlight and radio with me. Now I close the door. When the staff return in the morning, they'll find the lock forced, but nothing missing.

I step around the corner of the shack. At the far end of the beach, the road from Port Cymos begins to climb a rocky bluff inland. From there, the road winds higher to approach the hotel from behind.

A vehicle has stopped to let two men out. First the figures walk toward me, then break into a run. Headlights on, the car accelerates up the hill. They're going to try for a vertical envelopment. Two men to take me on the beach, two to cut off my escape at the top.

It doesn't take a genius to figure out what happened. When the pirates lost track of me, they had to figure out where I had come from. I could only have come from one of three places. Another ship in the harbor, the docks of the commercial port, or from the recreational port. There's too much activity in the commercial port to allow me to swim out to the *Goliath* undetected.

That left the recreational port. There are pleasure craft and yachts moored in the recreational port. The *Goliath* has not been in port long. The pirates would have eliminated the vessels that were present before they arrived. They likely sent teams to check out the yachts I might have used for a base. But one option dominated all the others—the Golden Paradise Hotel. A base I could have flown into unobserved from the sea.

The pirate captain's no slouch. He figured I had a boat hidden somewhere. Probably on the spit that separated the two chambers of the harbor. I would have to swim from *Goliath* to the spit. From there, return to the hotel. They raced around the curve of the harbor and made for the Golden Paradise. Arrived just in time to see me come out of the rental shack.

I rush to the elevator control box and hit the call button. There's a whine from above, and the cage begins to descend. I reach for the waterproof bag on my belt and draw the Mark 23. Turn to face my attackers.

Running in sand is no fun, but they're doing a good job. They'll cover the beach from the road to the elevator in under a minute. They'll reach me long before the elevator cage. I turn and sprint for the stone stairs I descended earlier that evening. Climb them two at a time.

Quads burning, I look back. I'm halfway up and the men have reached the base of the cliff. Without hesitation, one man mounts the stairs and climbs after me. The other stands on the beach, raises a pistol, and fires.

The crack of the pistol shot is lost in the wind. There's a muzzle flash, and the bullet smacks into the stone cliff behind me. I throw myself against the iron rails of the elevator gantry. Point the Mark 23 at the man on the beach and return fire.

A bullet strikes sparks from the girder next to me and I flinch away. The man on the stairs is firing.

It can't be easy to hit a man in a black wetsuit climbing steps against a black cliff. But I'll be a slow-moving target, presenting my back to the pirates. I squeeze between the iron girders, ducking under the cross-pieces. More bullets clang against the metal.

The whine of the electric winch grows louder. I look up, stare at the shadow of the elevator cage descending. If I lean too far inside the gantry, it'll tear me in half. I shrink against a girder as the elevator descends past me. The empty glass cage passes like an elongated bell jar. The stainless steel frame gleams like polished chrome on a fifties Thunderbird convertible.

I let instinct take over and step onto the roof of the cage. As calmly as stepping off a curb. The car carries me toward the man on the steps.

The pirate is looking high and low, left and right. He can't see me on the elevator roof. Thinks I'm still hiding behind the girders thirty feet above. The elevator draws even with him on the steps. I raise the Mark 23 and level it at his face.

"Hey."

The pirate jerks his head and stares at me. In that instant, his eyes widen and I pull the trigger. The .45 hollow point punches a black hole in the bridge of his nose. The flesh of his face ripples and flattens as the bones crack. The corpse pitches backward, falls from view as the elevator continues its descent.

Now what? The gunman at the bottom steps away from the base of the elevator to see what's going on. I fire twice. The pirate cringes and scurries back to the base of the gantry.

The elevator touches down with a gentle bump. The man

dodges inside. With a whine, the elevator starts back toward the top of the cliff. There's a metallic clang, and a bullet tears through the ceiling of the elevator at my feet. I step to one side, cling to the steel suspension cable. If he's using one of the *Goliath*'s USPs, that's 9mm NATO ball ammunition. Fast round, high penetration, low stopping power.

I point my Mark 23 at the bullet hole. The ceiling of the elevator is a circle with a diameter of at least seven feet. I'm conscious the other two pirates are in a car driving hell-for-leather on the twisting road that snakes toward the hotel. It's not an easy drive, but the clock is ticking and they could beat us to the top.

Halfway up, the elevator tilts precariously. The pirate has opened the front doors and is trying to climb out to get an angle on me. Gutsy move. There's only a couple of feet clearance between the elevator walls and the gantry. I rode the elevator a couple of times this morning. There's an inch-wide metal lip at the base. He's trying to edge out of the door with his feet planted sideways on that lip. One hand on the doorjamb for support, the other gripping his pistol.

There's a screech as the edge of the elevator frame scrapes the ribs of the gantry. A shower of sparks glitters against the cliff face. The man's weight has unbalanced the cage. Swearing, he climbs back inside.

We're almost at the top. I don't want to get caught in a crossfire between this guy and the pirates in the car. I grab the elevator cable with my left hand. Surely I can support my weight long enough with one arm. I cross my ankles around the cable, lean back, and point the Mark 23 at the connector between the cable and the elevator roof.

I fire once, twice, three times. The first shot misses and

punches a hole in the steel. The second strikes the cable and glances off. The third round does the trick. I don't see the round go in. All I see is the cable snap, a foot above the connector.

Free of the elevator's weight, the cable practically jerks my arm out of its socket. I hold on for dear life, watch the elevator plunge. At first, it falls in slow motion, then it picks up speed, The man inside doesn't scream. I wonder what it's like, if he's experiencing negative G's.

There's a puff of black-and-white dirt at the base of the gantry, followed by the sickening sound of a car crash. The awful sound of metal and glass exploding with an impact that fuses the inanimate materials of the structure with human meat and bone.

I shove the Mark 23 back in the bag, reach up with my free hand, and grasp the cable. Stretch out a leg to make certain I can reach the gantry. Brush the iron with the toe of my moccasin like I'm pedaling a bike. Then I grasp one of the cross-pieces as I'm hauled past. I let go of the cable and wrap my arms around the steel girder.

Look up, watch the end of the loose cable shine in the moonlight that flickers past the openings in the gantry. I have another fifteen feet to cover before I reach the clifftop. I swing myself from the gantry back onto the steps.

Every muscle and bone in my body aches. I stagger to the top, survey the tableau. The Golden Paradise Hotel is two hundred yards west of the elevator. The structure is a sprawling building, two stories. One cement path leads from the elevator to the veranda. Another, trimmed with a guard rail, winds along the edge of the cliff. Coin-operated binocular telescopes stand every thirty or forty feet.

The hotel looks peaceful, quiet and inviting. The wind

and distance from the hotel have kept staff and guests from hearing the shots or the crash of the elevator.

I jog toward the hotel. Turn my head at the snarl of a car's engine. The other two pirates have arrived in their vehicle, a Mercedes four-door sedan. They stop on the road a hundred yards away, turn their headlights on me, and dismount.

My hand goes into the plastic bag, reaching for the Mark 23. I expect shots. Instead, the men stand next to the car and watch me. I can't make out their features. They are black silhouettes in the glare of the headlights. One man is of average build. The other is bigger. Instinctively, I know he is the man who interrupted me on the *Goliath*. The pirate captain.

The hotel's front driveway faces away from the cliff. The best rooms have an ocean view. Without taking my hand from the butt of the Mark 23, I stride to the hotel. Walk around the back. I walk past a gazebo that sits on the lawn between the hotel and the cliff.

My suite is on the ground floor. Its French doors swing wide onto a terrace that overlooks the Aegean. The windows set in the doors are covered from the inside with wooden blinds.

Stein and Ash Harding-James are on the same floor. Stein and I face the ocean, Harding-James is on the other side. Our rooms are dark. We agreed that they would wait for me in the hotel bar. I enter my suite from the terrace and lock the French doors. Keep the blinds closed and the sitting room lights off. I go into the toilet, close the door, and turn on the light. Strip off my wetsuit, change into casual clothes. Khaki pants and a sports shirt. I stuff the Mark 23 into my waistband and pull the shirt down over it. Open a drawer and take out two spare magazines. Squeeze them into my hip pocket.

I run my fingers through my hair. Stare into my eyes in the mirror. Make sure I'm presentable. Yeah, I'm all there. I reach into the waterproof bag and retrieve my survival radio and the micro-SD card. The radio, I slip into my other hip pocket. The card, I tuck into my palm, clench my fist around it.

Time for a stiff drink.

3

THE SECOND DAY – EARLY MORNING, PORT CYMOS

The Seaview bar adjoins the main dining room of the Golden Paradise. It shares wraparound picture windows with the hotel's restaurant. Floor-to-ceiling, overlooking the Aegean. There is a mezzanine level, a main floor, and sliding doors that open to a wide terrace for outdoor dining.

The Long Bar separates the restaurant from the Seaview. It's Zinc-topped and stretches a mile. Barmen and barmaids are dressed in creased black trousers, white long-sleeved shirts, and black bow ties. They work back to back.

Circular tables are scattered across the Seaview at discreet distances from one another. The ceiling is mirrored. Candles flicker on the glass tops, giving the impression that the entire room is adrift in an ocean of lights.

The restaurant and bar space is center-fed. What that means, from a close quarters combat perspective, is that people enter the space through a front entrance in the middle of one long wall—the one opposite the picture windows. The kitchen is behind a set of swinging doors on one side of the Seaview.

Stein and Ash Harding-James are sitting at a table next to the picture windows. Stein, slender and pale in her signature black suit, straightens and catches my eye. I tilt my head in the direction of the kitchen and walk to a table. I sit with my back to the picture windows. From there, I can view the main entrance and the kitchen doors. If we're attacked through the main doors, we can escape through the kitchen. If we're attacked from the kitchen, we can escape through the main doors.

I signal a waitress and ask for a bottle of bourbon. Stein and Harding-James join me. Stein's body is all long, clean lines and subtle curves. She dresses like a model for a high-end women's fashion magazine. Her jacket is custom-tailored, cut to conceal a SIG P226 legion in a skeleton holster. A small, black briefcase dangles from two long, elegant fingers. It's just the right size for a small laptop.

There's a nervous chemistry between us. An attraction recognized but never acted on. Stein, a competent intelligence professional, is a shy, coltish girl. I don't know how well we would get on in bed. Don't know if such an encounter would hurt our working relationship.

Ash Harding-James is the opposite of Stein. He's a tall Englishman, a shade over six feet. He carries a few extra pounds, but his tailored Savile Row suit hides them well. They join me at the table, carrying their drinks. Scotch whiskey for Harding-James, a gin and tonic for Stein.

Stein eyes me suspiciously. "Have you got something against a nice ocean view?"

"Of course not," I say. "But we might have company."

"Is it the *Medusa*?" Stein asks.

The *Medusa*. A six-thousand-ton freighter in the *Goliath*'s class. The vessel went missing thirty-six hours ago with thirty tons of gold aboard. From anomalous transponder data, Stein developed a theory that the *Medusa* was hijacked, then repainted, reflagged, and renamed the *Goliath*. The ship then steamed to Port Cymos, a kind of nautical *Purloined Letter*, hidden in plain sight.

"No, it's the *Goliath*. There's no gold aboard, but she's definitely up to no good."

I tell Stein and Harding-James what I found. That the pirate crew tried to kill me, and may well burst in at any moment. I hold the micro-SD card between thumb and fore-finger, hand it to Stein.

"This was in the bridge laptop," I tell her. "No hard drive, so it's probably got the digital log on it. I have photos of the manual log, and photos of their GPS and transponder equipment. It looked like they had two of everything. Enough to spoof *their* location and that of the *Medusa*."

Western powers have been sanctioning Cuba, Venezuela, Iran and China for years. The Ukraine war has added Russia to the list of countries in our doghouse. Cargoes of choice are oil, refined petroleum products, and grain. Sanctions evaders are masters of electronic warfare.

In the simplest case, a vessel can simply turn off its transponder and vanish. However, this is risky because vessels over a certain size are required to keep their transponders on. While brief loss of transponder signal occurs frequently due to atmospheric disturbance or electronic glitches, extended transponder silence looks suspicious.

To avoid such surveillance, sanctions evaders have developed sophisticated tools and techniques to spoof transponder signals. It is possible to make a ship disappear, or make it appear to be where it is not. It is not unusual for a ship to appear to be steaming off Cape Horn when it is actually in Venezuela loading sanctioned oil or cocaine. In a high-profile case, a cargo ship steaming from Guyana to Gdansk was suspected of smuggling a cargo of cocaine picked up in Venezuela. The ship developed engine trouble in the Irish Sea. It was boarded by Irish Special Forces and impounded in Cork. The untold story was that electronic surveillance showed the ship steaming in circles off the coast of Guyana. In fact, it was somewhere else loading a cargo of drugs. When the vessel resumed normal transponder transmission and began its journey across the Atlantic, the authorities tracked its every move.

"I'll get the team on it right away," Stein says. "Upload the photos to the Company cloud."

Stein opens her laptop on the table, pushes the micro-SD card into a port. I upload the photos from the *Goliath*, and Stein uploads an image of the card. She takes out her survival radio. We both use these dual-mode devices instead of mobile phones. Stein taps out a message to her team in DC.

The waitress brings me a glass and a bottle of Bourbon. I offer some to Stein and Harding-James, but they shake their heads. Pour myself a stiff three fingers and gulp it down. I can still taste foul harbor water. Pour myself another, swirl the sweet, fiery liquor in my mouth before swallowing.

Harding-James clears his throat. "If that ship is not the *Medusa*, what do you think happened?"

I stare at our reflections in the picture windows. Behind the glass, lines of surf are visible on the beach. Silver moonlight glitters on the surface of the ocean. I can barely make out a hint of the spit of land that separates us from the commercial harbor. Behind it, the lights of ships are sprinkled like a field of stars. One of those lights is the *Goliath*. What happened? That's a good question. I cast my mind back twenty-four hours. Stein phoned to tell me an Englishman had come to her with an interesting puzzle.

ASH HARDING-JAMES IS the reason we're on Rhodes. He's the reason I boarded the *Goliath* and nearly got killed. He's one of the wealthiest Names in Lloyd's of London's insurance market. Stein arranged for us to meet at French's, an exclusive restaurant in DC. Harding-James gave us an introduction to the shipping market and insurance.

Lloyd's Names contribute money to syndicates that insure risks. Any risk that can be imagined can be insured. The risks of political elections, the risks of loss from fire or flood. In this particular case, the risk that a ship and its cargo might be lost. Lloyd's has been insuring marine risks for hundreds of years.

Harding-James explained that BRICS countries are experimenting with a new currency. The BRICS—Brazil, Russia, India, China, and South Africa—are tired of settling their trade in US dollars. Instead, they're settling their international transactions in their own national currencies. They plan to introduce their own BRICS currency, backed by gold. It's an aspiration that could take decades to realize. In the interim, they are experimenting with a system by which their trade balances—surpluses and deficits—are settled in gold. Gold flows from deficit countries to surplus countries. The high price of oil and gas ensures that Russia earns a trade surplus that approaches $1 trillion annually. As trade grows, the surplus will fall, but at the moment, the result is a massive influx of gold into Russia's coffers.

Gold is transported to Russia by rail, sea and air. The shipment vectors from deficit countries are randomized and kept secret. Details are jealously guarded. The *Medusa* was carrying thirty tons of gold bullion, 99.99% fine, from southeast Asia, across the Aegean, to the Russian port of Taganrog at the eastern tip of the Sea of Azov.

Ash Harding-James contributed $50 million of his own money to a syndicate to insure the gold cargo for $2 billion. The *Medusa*'s decrepit hull was insured by another syndicate for a measly $15 million.

The *Medusa* was meant to steam through the Suez Canal, enter the Aegean between Crete and Rhodes, travel up the Dodecanese Islands, through the Dardanelles, and into the Black Sea. Its transponder signals indicated that the ship steamed on course until it reached a point just past Kos. There, the signal was lost, and the *Medusa* disappeared.

When the vessel did not respond to repeated radio calls, the Hellenic Navy and Air Force mounted an air-sea rescue search. The weather was fine, and there was no reason for the *Medusa* to sink. The search focused on the position of last known contact, but no debris was found. The search radius was widened without result.

The Lloyd's underwriters were naturally concerned. Lloyd's used all its influence, all the information sources at its disposal, to find the *Medusa*. As the hours ticked by, the odds of finding the ship plunged.

Harding-James was the lead underwriter on the syndicate and had the most to lose. He called his friend, Jacob Stein, a private equity titan on Wall Street. Harding-James knew that Stein's daughter, Anya, was a senior executive at the Central Intelligence Agency. She had access to classified American signals intelligence and satellite data. Shouldn't the United States take an interest in $2 billion in gold bound for Russia?

Harding-James completed his introduction, and Stein took up the story.

The disappearance of the *Medusa* was the kind of mystery that brought out the nerd in Stein. Her father introduced her to Harding-James. She pulled all the signals intelligence and satellite data she could from the NSA, the CIA and DIA. She noticed two anomalies in the *Medusa's* transponder data. One interruption off Karpathos, halfway between Crete and Rhodes. Then, there was the final loss of signal at Kos.

The Hellenic Navy had that data. What the Greeks did not remark on were anomalies in the transponder signals of a second freighter, the *Goliath*. The *Goliath* was strikingly similar to the *Medusa*. Both were small, general cargo vessels of six thousand tons. The two ships were of comparable length and beam, which would render them difficult to distinguish by satellite imagery. When satellites look down on ships, all they have to go on are the ships' length, beam, and the color of their decks.

Stein noticed the *Goliath*, bound from Kavala, Greece, to Alexandria, Egypt. The *Goliath* exhibited a brief interruption in its transponder signal six hours after the *Medusa* disappeared. The anomaly occurred just before the *Goliath* reached Port Cymos.

There was no good reason for Stein to suspect the *Goliath*. All she knew was, other than the *Medusa*, no other ship in the Aegean experienced transponder interruptions that fateful night.

Stein theorized that the *Medusa* had been hijacked. That the pirates spoofed the track of the *Goliath* from Kavala to Kos. They then renamed, reflagged, and repainted the *Medusa* to make it look like the *Goliath*. They had it turn about on *Goliath*'s track toward Port Cymos. The *Goliath*'s false transponder track was interrupted only when the *Medusa* slipped into its place and began transmitting as the *Goliath*. The real *Goliath*, meanwhile, turned off its transponder and disappeared.

The data was sketchy, but Stein's theory was realistic. If she was right, some very clever and resourceful pirates had made off with $2 billion in gold, leaving Lloyd's on the hook. The stakes were high. People have been murdered for less.

Stein invited me to come with her and Harding-James to Port Cymos. The *Goliath* had been moored in the harbor for twenty-four hours. We could easily fly to Rhodes and check her out.

"This theory of yours is pretty thin," I told her.

"I'm right about *Goliath*. I know it."

Stein's a gambler. No one gets to be a Deputy Director of the CIA at thirty-five without taking risks. Her career was unconventional. Harvard Law, FBI, the Company. She took assignments no one else would take. Colombia, Ukraine, Afghanistan, Iraq. She went on operations with SEAL teams and Delta Force. DEVGRU and CAG. I've seen her perform.

When I left Delta, I took on executive protection roles and contract missions for the Company. I do a lot of work for Stein.

"It's an awful long way to go on a hunch."

"Come on, Breed. What do you have to lose? Greece, the Aegean, the romance, the finder's fee..."

"The finder's fee?"

"Sure. It's standard practice if you save the insurance company a big payout." Stein glanced at Harding-James.

"I'm sure we can work something out," the Englishman said.

"I don't need the money."

Stein held my eyes with hers. "But you *will* do it."

"Why?"

She put her hand on my forearm and leaned close.

"Because I'm asking you to. Because if I'm right, Harding-James and I will run into some very bad dudes all by ourselves."

The electricity of Stein's touch did it. She's tough, but there's a girlish naiveté about her. Especially when she's in nerd mode. I don't need the money, but I'm not immune to the promise of Greece, the Aegean, and... romance.

Here I am.

I SHIFT my gaze from Harding-James to Stein.

"I think you were half right," I tell her. "The *Goliath* is a pirate ship. Its track from Kavala was genuine. Had to be. Satellite photos would render the vessel easily identifiable in port. It sailed south and met the *Medusa* that night. East of Karpathos, west of Rhodes. A ruse—some kind of medical emergency—the pirates got aboard."

"The first *Medusa* anomaly," Stein says.

"Yes."

"The *Medusa* had a security detail," Harding-James says.

"Half a dozen former SEALs and Special Boat Service operators. All heavily armed."

"The pirates were also heavily armed, and they had the advantage of surprise. I think they overwhelmed the security detail and crew. Then they steamed the *Goliath* north to Kos, impersonating the *Medusa*."

Stein leans forward in her chair. "While the *Medusa* turned off its transponder and sailed elsewhere."

"Exactly. When the *Goliath*, impersonating the *Medusa*, reached Kos, it turned off the transponder it was using to impersonate *Medusa*. At that point, the world was deceived into thinking the *Medusa* disappeared. In fact, it had been seized six hours earlier."

Stein picks up on my theory. "The *Goliath* then turned back on its original course for Port Cymos and resumed transmitting its own transponder signal."

"And *that* cut-over created the anomaly you noticed in *Goliath*'s track. Your original theory was correct in principle. It only differs from *this* theory in terms of execution."

"But where's the *Medusa*?"

"Think about it. The *Medusa* and *Goliath* are comparable ships. They both make about fifteen knots, which is seventeen miles an hour. The *Medusa* had six hours from the time of the first anomaly to the loss of signal. That distance is our search radius. I make it a hundred miles."

"How much ocean do we have to search?"

I didn't go to college, but snipers are damn good at math. "The area of a circle. It's about thirty thousand square miles."

"Oh my God."

"You can see why they might have done it this way."

Stein stares at me. Realization comes over her features.

Harding-James looks blank. "The Hellenic Navy," Stein says, "is searching in the wrong place."

"It *could* be searching in the wrong place." I'm beginning to enjoy myself. "If the hijacking occurred west of Rhodes like we think, they are searching at the northern extreme of our search area."

"Let's call the police," Harding-James says.

I drain my second glass of Bourbon. Pour another. "No. We know about the *Goliath* now. Stein can have our satellites watch it."

Stein sips her G&T. Stares at her radio. "I could ask the Hellenic Navy to refocus their search."

I shake my head. "We're still operating on a hunch. If I'm right, the *Medusa* has gone to ground, and so has the crew that's taken her. They're busy transferring cargo now. That means they're well-hidden and fixed in place. I doubt an armada of search vessels and airplanes will find her. Let's narrow the search ourselves before involving anyone else."

"How are you going to cover a search area of thirty thousand square miles?"

"Let me think about it. Have your team work the data. That's what they do well. If they narrow the search area, we can cover it by helo."

"We have a problem," Harding-James says.

Stein and I face him.

"The pirates you encountered tonight are likely to try to kill you again. Nor will it be difficult for them to learn that Anya and I checked into the hotel at the same time you did. They'll try to kill all of us."

"Of course. What do you propose?"

"I have a friend on this island. Athanasios Kyrios, a Greek shipping magnate. He has an estate twenty miles west of here. A wonderful place called Ésperos. I think he will allow us to stay with him."

"That could help," Stein says, "if you think he'll agree."

"I'm sure he will. He also has his own security force, which could be helpful. Do we tell him our circumstances?"

"I don't think we have a choice," Stein says. "He'll be taking a risk by harboring us. It's not fair to keep him in the dark."

I shake my head. "It's not just a matter of fairness. If we want his help, he can't be effective unless he knows the story."

"Alright." Harding-James downs his drink. "I'll call him in the morning."

"One more thing." I rest my hand on the butt of the Mark 23 under my shirt. "We don't go back to our rooms tonight. We stay together, right here. Those people from the *Goliath* aren't playing games."

4

THE SECOND DAY – MORNING, PORT CYMOS

"**D**o you want anything else, sir?"
It's past closing time, and the restaurant has gone dark. Ours is the only table in the Seaview still occupied. The pretty waitress studies the bottle of Bourbon, which is only down by a quarter. I've been paying close attention to Stein's efforts to quarterback her team.

"No, thank you."

Stein looks up from her laptop. "Do you have room service?" she asks the girl.

"Yes, ma'am. Twenty-four hours."

"Can you bring us their menu, please. Ask them to serve us here."

"Of course, ma'am."

The waitress bows out and a young man brings us the room service menu. Stein orders soft drinks and a stack of club house sandwiches. Hands the boy a bunch of fifty-Euro notes. "Whatever we order, bill to my room," she says. "This is for you. Let me know when it runs out."

Stein is a machine. Runs ten miles every morning, swims

an hour every night. I don't think she sleeps. Right now, she's making notes in a leather-bound notebook. Her script is tiny and precise.

Harding-James, bleary-eyed, struggles awake like a man swimming to the surface from a great depth. He's taken off his jacket. Stein has kept her own jacket on, to conceal her weapon. The creases in her suit are blade-sharp.

"Any luck?" I ask.

Stein sets her Montblanc down on the notebook. "Right now we're defining the problem," she says.

"Tell me."

"All two hundred of the Dodecanese Islands are within our search area, and many of the Cyclades. We're looking at four hundred islands. Most of them uninhabited."

"All inside our thirty-thousand-square mile zone?"

"Yes." Stein clasps her hands behind her head and stretches. Her white shirt rides up and I catch a glimpse of her flat stomach. Her navel is an innie, four inches away from her SIG. She catches me looking, likes to tease. "The problem is more complicated than we thought. It's not a simple matter of square miles of ocean. It's more a question of miles of coastline. Thousands of miles, because each island has a coast. There are a whole bunch of rocks we're excluding. Also, islands smaller than a certain size. A lot depends on how the pirates plan to transport the stolen gold."

"Ship, road, or airplane."

"Yes. The larger islands with airports are high probability targets. I've already got satellites tasked to cover all of them. The *Medusa* would offload on the coast and they would transport the gold by road to an airport. Of course, it could be stored while the pirates lie low."

"It seems too simple."

"It *is* too simple, but we have to cover all the bases. I'm having the team review satellite imagery from the time the *Medusa* disappeared. Anything that looks like a ship tied up off one of our high probability islands."

Stein consults her notebook. "Then we have a set of second tier candidates. Islands with coastlines long enough and rugged enough to conceal a freighter the size of *Medusa*. These islands don't have an airport. But the *Medusa* could be unloading the gold for storage so it can be picked up later by another ship."

"I can understand a freighter avoiding detection from the sea, but not from the air. It doesn't look like they can camouflage a ship with foliage."

"I agree. Concealment from the air is unlikely, but possible. The Greek islands are volcanic. The Aegean and the Mediterranean have been eroding these coastlines for millennia. There are caves all over those coasts. *Caverns*."

"Big enough to conceal a six-thousand-ton freighter?"

Stein frowns. "Possibly. We can't rule it out."

"In that case, forget satellites and drones. We need to go in with a helo."

"Yes. We're searching for a needle in a haystack, and we have yet to find the haystack."

Silent, we stare at each other. Harding-James looks like he's about to nod off again.

"Oil tankers conduct mid-ocean transfers," I say.

"Mid-ocean transfer of the gold would take twelve hours. Based on the period between the first transponder anomaly and loss of signal, *Medusa* only had six. We're checking satellite imagery, but it's not a great bet. We have a drone reconnaissance unit at Souda Bay Navy Base. I've got one drone searching the Cyclades and another the coast of Crete."

Drones and satellites. As far as I can tell, Stein is trying everything short of refocusing the Hellenic Navy search. I want to know how she's going to narrow down our search area. "What about signals intelligence? Any suspicious transmissions?"

"I have the NSA monitoring everything. Blanket surveillance. All transmissions in the area. Telephone, VOIP, text, satellite communications. They are running a massive sweep for all communications that contain the words *Medusa* and *Goliath*. Independent or joint, alone or used with words like Cyclades, Crete, Dodecanese, Rhodes, Turkey, Turkiye, Dardanelles, Bosporus. Everything the team could think of. First, the AI will troll the results, then our team will use Mark One Eyeball."

I can't fault anything Stein's done. The modern equivalent of old reliable shoe leather.

Stein shakes her head. "We have wall-to-wall ISR—Intelligence, Surveillance, Reconnaissance. Nothing should get by us. Yet, so far, the *Medusa* has."

The young waiter rolls out a silver service on a white tablecloth. Obviously liberated from the main dining room. He sets porcelain plates before us, careful not to disturb Stein's laptop. He's obviously catering to her as he would royalty. With a flourish, he lifts the lid off the center plate. Reveals a stack of half a dozen club house sandwiches.

Stein grins. "I'm not doing this on an empty stomach."

The Company's Deputy Director looks like she's enjoying herself.

Dawn in the Greek islands is beautiful, but it depends on where you are. The Golden Paradise Hotel is on the northwest coast of Rhodes, and the island is oriented from southwest to northeast. That means that from the hotel, the orb of the rising sun is obscured by the bulk of the island. We get great views of the sunset.

The rising sun smears the sky with the color of rich salmon. A few wisps of cloud will burn away over the course of the morning. The sky has lightened from midnight blue in the west to a pastel hue in the east.

Stein and I leave Harding-James in the hotel lounge. In a couple of hours, he'll call his friend, Kyrios. Unlikely to reach the businessman with his first call, he might have to wait for a callback. I lead Stein outside and we stroll on the clifftop, following the guardrail.

"What happened over there?" Stein asks.

Police vehicles and an ambulance form a rough semicircle around the top of the stone steps. Uniformed men are inspecting the elevator's machine shed and taking photographs. More police gather on the beach and crowd around the elevator. The glass has been shattered and the steel frame bent. It looks like a bomb went off inside the cage.

"I guess the elevator had an accident."

"Did you have anything to do with it?"

"Of course not."

Stein frowns.

The cliff curves toward the elevator in a shallow arc. I turn one of the coin-operated telescopes. It rotates freely to cover the beach and much of the clifftop. I feed the mechanism some money and focus the telescope on my handiwork.

Ambulance attendants have joined the police on the beach. They carry a stretcher between them. One of the men points across the beach to the Port Cymos road. The other raises a phone to his ear.

The attendants want the ambulance to meet them at the road. I don't blame them. They're not about to carry the pirate's corpse up those stone steps on a stretcher. There are two bodies to carry out, and they'll have to make two trips. A bloody arm sticks out from the twisted wreckage. I turn the telescope to study the men on the clifftop.

Ambulance attendants on the clifftop get into their vehicle and drive back down the road. They follow the same route the pirate captain and his henchman took in their effort to cut me off.

A tall man dressed in casual clothes watches the police. He looks like a hotel guest, mildly curious about the activity. He's six-foot, sandy haired and fit. He wears slacks, a sport shirt, and deck shoes. A brown leather bag is slung over his shoulder and across his chest.

I recognize him from his posture, build, and profile.

"We have company."

Stein takes over the telescope, scans the cliff.

"Colonel Orlov," she says. "As I live and breathe."

"Russian gold, Russian operator. Shall we say hello?"

Colonel Maxim Orlov of the 45th Guards Spetznaz. Referred to in whispers as "the sword in Volodya's hand." I first met the colonel at the Battle of Debaltseve, eastern Ukraine, 2014. He was advising the Donbas militia. I was observing the Ukrainian army. Both sides shelled the city. Caught in a crossfire, Orlov and I independently found shelter in the same bombed-out basement. His English was better than my Russian, and we came to an uneasy truce. When the shelling ended, we went our separate ways.

Stein and I stroll over to Orlov. The Russian colonel turns at our approach and smiles. "Stein. Breed. Your work?"

"I was in bed all night," I tell him. "Slept like a baby."

"A likely story."

Stein cuts to the chase. "What brings *you* here, Colonel?"

"The same thing that has drawn yourselves." Orlov opens his leather bag and produces an eleven-by-fourteen-inch plastic envelope. Inside is a brown paper liner, containing a package an inch thick. "I have been tasked to deliver this package to you. My involvement is simply a matter of convenience. Because we have met, you will not doubt its provenance."

Stein accepts the package. "What's inside?"

"Satellite data," Orlov says, closing his bag. "Signals intelligence. Is there a place we can speak for a few minutes?"

We make our way to the gazebo behind the hotel. Sit together on a bench, Stein between myself and Orlov.

"A distinction, if I may," Orlov says. "It's not our gold."

"It's bound for Taganrog."

"Title does not pass to the Russian Federation until we sign for the gold upon delivery." Orlov leans back. Assumes a casual pose. "Until then, it is the property of the deficit countries. It is they who have purchased the insurance."

Stein turns the package over in her hands. "Why all this?"

"Of course, we take an interest in the shipment. We tracked the *Medusa* through the Suez Canal, into the Mediterranean. Not with one satellite, but many. An entire network."

"That's more than we did," Stein says.

"Don't feel bad, Stein. You had no special interest in the *Medusa*. You've arrived late to the game through no fault of your own."

"You know where the ship is."

"Sadly, no. But we *can* narrow down your search. It's possible to track a ghost ship by satellite and signals intelligence. We use a network of satellites to triangulate its AIS— Automatic Identification System—transponder signals. But these can be disguised. We also track other microwave emissions. The ship's weather radar, for example. There is nothing new here. America has this capability. You would have it had you been alerted sooner."

"You wouldn't let us have anything truly secret."

"Of course not. We can do much more, as we have proven in combat. *This* data, however, will catch you up."

I search Orlov's eyes. They are a piercing blue. "Why?"

"You are working for Lloyd's of London."

"What's that got to do with it?"

Stein relaxes. "The Russians want the insurance company to find the gold," she says, "not the European Union."

"Brava, Stein." Orlov beams. "If you find the gold, the insurance company keeps its money, the gold is returned to its owners, who complete shipment to us. If you *don't* find it, Lloyd's pays out, the deficit countries buy more gold and ship it to us. The insurance company loses. *But* if the *Greeks* find it and say nothing, two billion dollars will find its way into some bourgeoisie European Union slush fund."

"Is that the only reason?" I ask. "Spite?"

"Isn't that enough? Western countries have profited

enough at our expense." Orlov places his hands on his knees and rises. "Now I must go. My role here is finished."

Stein and I watch Orlov stride briskly to the hotel parking lot.

"Do you believe him?" Stein asks.

"I do. His story hangs together."

"Alright," Stein says. "Let's go inside and see what we have."

I LEAD Stein back to the Seaview, claim the table we occupied last night. The staff have opened the doors to the terrace and a fresh breeze ruffles Stein's dark hair. The air smells of salt, and I hear the faint whisper of waves on the beach below.

The same young man who served us last night approaches. Day staff are rolling in. The restaurant and bar in the midst of a shift change.

We order coffee and breakfast sandwiches. Stein offers the boy more Euros. He shakes his head and beams. "That is not necessary, ma'am. I am still... how do you say? *Recovering* from your generosity."

Stein opens the plastic envelope and sets the contents on the table. The material has been organized into three smaller stacks. Photographs, transponder data, and signals intelligence. We examine each in turn.

The photographs are only mildly interesting. There are black-and-white pictures of the *Medusa* transiting the Suez Canal. More pictures crossing the Mediterranean. A separate set of photographs show the *Goliath* in port at Kavala. Photos of the vessel crossing the Aegean, then mooring in Port

Cymos. No new information here. What is remarkable is the similarity between the *Medusa* and the *Goliath*. Same length, same beam, same number of masts and cargo hatches. The two could be sister ships. That strikes me as unusual for ships so old.

I point out the similarity to Stein.

"Both vessels were built in Skaramagas, Greece." Stein checks her notes. "Fifteen years apart. There were three dozen built of the class, so the resemblance is not unusual. It was a common enough design before larger container ships took over most of the trade. Ships like *Medusa* and *Goliath* are still useful for short-haul general cargo transport."

"Who owns them?"

"Two brass-plate companies. One in Panama, one in the UAE. The *Medusa* sails under the Panamanian flag, the *Goliath* is Liberian. This isn't unusual. The international shipping business is completely opaque. Brass-plate companies, often without mailing addresses, are set up to own a single vessel. The companies are then embedded in an obscure network of shadow companies offshore. It is almost impossible to trace beneficial ownership. Ownership resides in countries different from the countries of registry."

"And Lloyd's insures ships and cargoes under such conditions?"

"So long as the premiums roll in. Lloyd's often makes payment under the same conditions, with few, if any, questions asked."

We set aside the photographs and troll through the transponder data.

"It isn't very different from the data I already have," Stein says.

"Were you expecting it to be?"

"No. I've saved the best for last."

Stein sets the photos and the transponder data aside. Together, we examine the signals intelligence.

"This is the real thing," Stein says. "Weather radar. Satellite communications. HF radio transcripts. You can see how the signals intelligence continues after the first transponder anomaly."

"Albeit at a reduced volume. There's heavy radio traffic all the way to the Karpathos-Rhodes gap. After the first transponder anomaly, the signals intelligence falls off. It disappears completely after the transponder goes dark."

"Can you read the coordinates of these data points?"

"I think so. The spoofed transponder signals head north to Kos. It looks like these weather radar signals trace a path due west."

"Toward Crete." Stein straightens in her chair. "I think Orlov's cut our search area in half."

"At least. Can you have your team synthesize this data for us?"

"Yes." Stein stands, arranges the material on the table, and scans it with her phone. "I'll have them prepare a complete report."

I stare out the picture windows. Sails have begun to dot the Aegean. Slow is fast. Scrambling search and rescue assets south will just create confusion and spook the pirates. Narrowing the search area will permit a more focused effort.

Orlov's package makes it clear the Russians were all over the *Medusa*. The detail in their satellite photographs was stunning. It's hard to imagine the freighter sitting undetected off an island's coast.

Could the pirates really fit the *Medusa* into a cave? Possibly, but only if they chop the masts off. Of course, that can be done. By now, the shell of the *Medusa* is expendable. The pirates aren't going to think twice about lopping off its masts.

"What are you lot up to? Sitting here, thick as thieves."

It's Harding-James. The big Englishman eases himself into a chair.

"Narrowing down the search," Stein tells him. "Have you spoken to Kyrios?"

"Indeed I have." Harding-James looks thoroughly self-satisfied. "He'll send a car round after lunch."

I glance at Stein.

"The team's working around the clock," she says. "No one sleeps until we have a report."

5

THE SECOND DAY – AFTERNOON, ÉSPEROS

We stand outside the Golden Paradise, our luggage set on the flagstones. I'm carrying my usual duffel bag. Stein's got her briefcase and a small, hard-shell carry-on. Harding-James's suitcase is the size of a steamer trunk.

"Got enough room in there?" I ask.

"Most of the items a traveling gentleman requires."

We turn around at the throaty roar of a high-performance engine. An overpowered Bentley Bentayga SUV races toward us on the Port Cymos road. I take a step back and my hand hovers close to the butt of my Mark 23. The Bentley turns into the hotel drive without slowing, screeches to a stop inches from Harding-James's trunk.

The young woman who steps out from behind the wheel is... breathtaking. Five-foot-eight. Not beautiful, but attractive. Soft features, rosy cheeks, a sensual mouth stiff with determination. Her curls bounce, long and wild, the color of rust.

She looks us up and down, assesses the situation. Goes to

Harding-James and extends her hand. "It's good to see you, Ash."

"It's good to see you, Hecate."

The young woman turns to me and Stein. "I'm Hecate Kyrios. I told my father I would drive your party to Ésperos."

She *told* her father. He didn't *ask* her. She didn't volunteer.

"That's very kind of you, Ms Kyrios," Stein says.

"Call me Hecate." She pronounces it Hey-kah-tee. "You must be Stein and Breed."

"A pleasure to meet you," I say.

Hecate picks up my duffel and Stein's carry-on, one in each hand. Pops the Bentley's hatchback and throws the luggage onto the cargo bed. "There isn't enough room for your trunk," she tells Harding-James. "We'll have the hotel send it on."

The girl-woman walks around the SUV, opening the passenger doors. She studies me. Evaluates my capacity for hard physical exercise. "Mr Breed, you can sit with me in front."

How nice of her.

A four-door Mercedes sedan appears in the distance. Races toward the hotel. My stomach tightens. "We've got company."

"Don't mind them," Hecate says.

We pile into the Bentley. "Who are they?"

"My bodyguards."

Hecate floors the gas. The Bentley's V-8 accelerates the vehicle from zero to sixty in four seconds. I'm punched back into my seat before I can reach for the lap belt.

"Do you have a first name, Breed?"

"Yes."

The girl peels out of the drive in a high-speed racing drift. Straightens the vehicle and accelerates to eighty miles an hour.

"Have we reached the end of the runway yet?" I fasten my lap belt.

"I prefer a lower center of gravity," Hecate says. "This is my father's car."

"This isn't the coast road."

"I don't like driving through the city," Hecate says. Her hands grip the wheel at ten and two, her arms straight, race-driver style. Her blue eyes never leave the road. "We'll take the mountain roads."

I check the passenger's rearview mirror. The hotel is disappearing into the distance. So are Hecate's bodyguards.

Greece is mountainous, and Rhodes is no exception. I don't think there's a single straight highway on the island. The only straight stretch of concrete I've seen since our arrival has been the airport runway outside Rhodes City.

Hecate slows on the twisting road, barely wide enough for two cars. It's bordered by rocky mountainsides and steep drops. The Bentley is a classy SUV, designed to show off in fashionable London neighborhoods. This model has been customized, equipped with a manual transmission, and is built to perform. Hecate accelerates on the straights, brakes before the turns, and accelerates coming out. She works the brakes, clutch and gearshift like a professional. I don't know how the Bentley's transmission can take this much punishment.

"You drive like a man."

Hecate smiles. "I won the Acropolis Rally two years ago."

"You've driven this route before."

"Yes." Hecate glances at her watch. She's timing herself.

I decide to test her. "How many times do you shift gears on this route?"

Hecate answers without missing a beat. "One-hundred-and-forty-seven-point-two times over six miles."

"Point two?"

"It's an average."

Hecate slows as we fly through the main street of a small village. Once outside the populated center, she opens up on a rare straight. Craggy vineyards flash by on either side. "The local *chima* wine is very good. The vintners share their product with my father. A number will come to the party tonight."

"What's the occasion?"

Going into a turn, Hecate applies the brakes. The stretch is behind us. Once again, we careen over twisting mountain roads. "It's my birthday. Today, I am twenty-seven."

Hecate accelerates coming out of the curve. A hundred yards ahead, a silver Citroën has slewed across the road. A man stands in front, waving for us to stop. It looks like a breakdown, a man asking for help.

No way. I see movement on the craggy hillside to the right. Two men behind a stand of stunted pine trees.

There's no time to think at times like this. People don't rise to the occasion. They fall to the level of their training, and training is automatic. Hecate's vehicle is traveling eighty-eight feet per second. We're going to cover the distance to the roadblock in three seconds. The prescribed course of action is to touch the brake, point the car at the front corner of the roadblock vehicle, then accelerate through. The impact will spin the enemy vehicle around and disable its engine.

Hecate stamps on the brake, holds the Bentley in a

straight line. We're two-thirds of the way to the roadblock.
The man in front of us sees we're not going to stop in time.
He turns to run toward his friends.

I reach over, grab the wheel with both hands, and twist it
hard right. Hecate's foot is still on the brake and the Bentley
slews sideways. The air is filled with the screech of tires skid-
ding on pavement. We smash into the Citroën with the
explosive crash of two metal objects coming together at
thirty miles an hour. The man is caught between the two
cars. His face smacks into Hecate's window and a gout of
blood spurts from his nose and mouth. Squeezed from his
crushed body like ketchup from a sachet.

Hecate's not hurt, she's stunned. The Bentley's stalled.
"Start the car," I tell her. "Get going."

My voice steadies the girl. She looks at me, turns the key
in the ignition, and throws the car into gear. "Around," I tell
her. "Go around."

The rattle of submachine gun fire echoes from the slope
above. Two rounds smack into the windshield between my
head and Hecate's. Bullets riddle the Bentley's hood. The
engine roars. Standard 9mm NATO ball hasn't a chance
against an engine block.

I draw my Mark 23, fire through the windshield. Double-
action, long first pull. The first round punches a hole in the
plexiglass and I keep firing. My .45 caliber hollow points have
little penetrating power, but the first three rounds expand and
make a hole big enough to shoot through. Chips of bark fly from
the trunk of the pine shielding the gunmen. One man drops his
weapon and lifts his hands to his face. Pitches backwards.

Hecate guides the Bentley around the Citroën. The body
of the man she hit slides to the ground. His head and neck

are intact, but the rest of him has been squashed flat. Like a leaf preserved between the pages of a book. His body and the side of the sedan are a slick brown mass.

The gunmen are armed with MP5s. Notorious for their extremely high rates of fire. They dumped their mags on us in seconds. The remaining gunman is reloading. "Let's go," I say. "Show us what this baby can do."

Pop, pop, pop. Stein's got her window down. Fires her SIG to keep the gunman cowering. Hecate floors the gas and the powerful 4.0-liter V-8 jerks the mass of the vehicle forward. The Bentley explodes away from the roadblock.

The gunman dumps his second mag at the rear of our fleeing Bentley. Hecate's a born racing driver. In seconds, we're out of sight behind the next curve.

"Dear God," Harding-James breathes. "They might have killed us."

"Men have tried to kidnap me before," Hecate says.

"Do you really think this was a kidnap attempt?" Harding-James asks.

"That man wanted us to stop. The others would have come out and held us at gunpoint."

I don't think so. There are no coincidences. Had we stopped, we'd all be dead.

Hecate drives only a little slower than when we left the hotel. She must be shaken by the experience, but she covers it well.

A ringtone sounds from the dash. Hecate's mobile phone has been clipped to a hands-free cradle. She reaches forward and pushes a button. "*Ne?*"

A torrent of Greek issues from the phone. Hecate responds in rapid fire. The initial exchange involves her answering questions. The conversation ends with her instructing the man on the other end.

Hecate disconnects the call.

"My bodyguards have come upon the ambush," she says. "Two gunmen are dead, the third has run away. I have instructed them to dispose of the bodies, then join us at Ésperos."

"How did the third man escape?" Stein asks.

"The vehicle they used for the roadblock was drivable," Hecate says. "He took the car and drove past our men on his way east. Driving on the right side of the road, they did not see the damage to the side of his car."

"We can't disguise the damage to *this* car."

Smears of blood decorate the outside surface of Hecate's side window.

"We shall be in Ésperos in short order. My bodyguards have called ahead, my father has been informed. This vehicle will be kept in a covered garage. No one will notice."

THE INTERIOR of Rhodes is the most disorganized landscape I've ever seen. It's more disorganized than Afghanistan. Miles of winding roads and trails meander over the rocky hillsides without rhyme or reason.

We crest a hill, and all of Rhodes and the Aegean spread below us. To the left we see the sweep of the island and look down on hilltop settlements and ruins.

"That's Monolithos to the left," Hecate says. "Ésperos is straight ahead."

I follow Hecate's gaze and find myself staring at a sprawling compound high on a cliff. The area on the clifftop would cover a dozen football fields. It's bordered on three sides by a tall, white wall. A Bell Huey helicopter sits on a helipad. Mounted on a pole, an orange and white wind sock flutters. The estate overlooks a thin crescent of white beach. From this distance, I make the beach two hundred yards long, flanked on either side by rocky bluffs. There's a speck on the blue ocean—a white yacht moored a hundred yards off the beach.

"That helicopter flew me into Ésperos this morning," Hecate says. "That yacht is my father's. The *Grigoro Fidi*. It's his pride and joy."

Close to the cliff edge, the estate is dominated by a sprawling blue-and-white painted building. It must be the main residence. Smaller outbuildings stand between the residence and the helipad. Those must be for staff and other utilities.

It takes us ten minutes to descend the twisting road to the Kyrios estate. The main gate is constructed from thick steel bars. A gray Land Rover has been pulled in front, blocking the entrance.

A man steps from behind the Land Rover and lifts a hand. I can't tell if it's a greeting or a signal to stop. Probably both. He's wearing a white linen suit and a black tie. The jacket is roomy enough to conceal a pistol in a cross-draw holster at his left hip.

Hecate exchanges words with the man. He studies the damage on the driver's side with a critical eye. Ducks his head for a look at me, Stein and Harding-James. Satisfied, he straightens and calls out to men standing behind the gate.

A man sitting in the Land Rover starts the engine and drives forward to clear the gate. Other men swing the butterfly gates open and Hecate drives through. As we pass,

I notice the men carry M4 carbines slung across their chests.

I look in the passenger's rearview mirror. Now that we're inside, the men close the gates, and the Land Rover reverses into place. It would take a determined attack with a vehicle-borne IED to penetrate that defense.

Straight ahead, the road leads to a driveway in front of the main residence. To the right is a spacious parking lot.

"The guests haven't arrived yet," Hecate says. "We have an hour before they get here."

The road curves left. Hecate steers toward a low building that looks like a garage.

It is. A man in jeans and white shirt touches a button, and the door opens with a rattle of metal slats. Hecate pulls into the lighted interior and parks the car.

I expected to see expensive sports cars, but I'm disappointed. There is a silver Rolls Royce Phantom sedan, two more Bentley Bentayga SUVs, four Land Rovers, and a jeep. The rugged terrain of Rhodes does not lend itself to fancy sets of wheels. I doubt the Phantom sees much use, and then, only on the flat coast roads.

The man pops open the hatchback and hauls out our luggage. We step outside the garage and he closes the door.

Hecate strides toward the big house. Up close, I can see that the side facing the cliff is spanned by a wide terrace. Blue-and-white painted wooden rails have been decorated with long flower boxes. The terrace is set with tables, each covered with white cloth. A live band is setting up its instruments in one corner.

Athanasios Kyrios steps from the front door, greets us with open arms. He ignores Harding-James's offer of a handshake.

Hugs the Englishman and touches his face affectionately with both hands. "Ash, my dear, dear friend! It is good to see you! You had trouble on the road. Not my daughter's crazy driving?"

"No, Thanos." Harding-James returns the hug, disengages himself. "I'm afraid it was those pirates who made an attempt on Breed's life last night."

"It looked like a kidnap attempt," Hecate says.

Kyrios shakes his head. "No, my dear. You will learn, there are no coincidences in life."

Hecate smiles. "What of fate, Father? Destiny?"

"That is something else," Kyrios says. "That is the will of the gods."

Kyrios is an average-looking man, not much taller than his daughter. A strong man, with a broad chest and shoulders. His hair is silver, cut short. The fur on his muscular forearms still bears a hint of Hecate's copper. Early sixties, a bit soft around the middle, but energetic. He wears a white short-sleeved dress shirt and a bright blue tie.

The man is unpretentious, but exudes charm and magnetism. He takes Stein's hand in both of his. "Ah, the beautiful Ms Stein. May I call you Anya? Of course, you will not object. I am Thanos."

I've never seen Stein flustered. She actually blushes. Hecate meets my eyes over her father's shoulder. She looks amused.

The old man turns to me, takes my hand. "Mr Breed. I have heard much about you. You have been on our island but a short time, and have managed to kill four men." Kyrios's grip is an iron vise. He's careful not to crush my hand. This man hasn't spent his life shuffling paper.

I haven't told anyone about the man I killed on the

Goliath. He makes five, but who's counting? "I reckon I took care of three. Your Bentley killed the fourth."

The old man laughs heartily. Puts one arm around my shoulders and another around Hecate's. Pulls us close. "He was stupid enough to stand in the way of a woman driver."

Hecate cringes at her father's old-school sexism.

"I think he was foolish to stand in the way of a Kyrios," I say.

Kyrios releases Hecate and plants both meaty paws on my shoulders. "Listen to him," he says. "Be careful, Breed. I am starting to like you."

Hecate holds the front door open and Kyrios leads us into the house. Hecate allows me to precede her. Puts a hand on my shoulder and squeezes gently. "You like my father already, don't you? He has nothing but friends."

"Theo will take your bags to your rooms," Kyrios says. "Please go upstairs and freshen up. Ash, my friend. The hotel says your things will be here in half an hour."

The vast terrace is separated from the interior of the house by floor-to-ceiling glass doors that slide open on rails. I feel ocean breeze on my face. Servants dressed in black trousers and white jackets are carrying food from the kitchen to the terrace.

"You have picked the perfect time to arrive at Ésperos." Kyrios spreads his arms to encompass the whole of the house. "It is Hecate's birthday, and we are having a party. It will give us a chance to demonstrate our hospitality."

There's a stone fireplace all of ten feet wide against one wall. The mantel sports photographs of Kyrios and his family. There are recent color photographs. Black-and-white photographs from the fifties and sixties. Sepia-toned prints that date to the Second World War and before.

One color photograph is of Kyrios and Hecate standing together on a lawn in front of what looks like a British college. Hecate is wearing a graduation gown. "That's my graduation at Cambridge," Hecate says.

"Is that where you learned to speak English?"

"No, my father sent me to an international school before Queens' College."

Another color photograph is of a beautiful woman with long brown hair. This was taken in the eighties. It's funny how you can tell when a photograph was taken by the quality of the color. It must have something to do with the changes in the paper and chemical process. The resemblance to Hecate is striking.

"That's my mother," Hecate says. "She lives in Athens."

Kyrios's second wife. They must be divorced or separated, but I don't want to pry. "Do you live in Athens?"

"Yes. I run the family's island ferry monopoly, coastal freight, and tramp charters."

"Do tramp freighters still exist?"

Hecate laughs. "Oh yes, it is a growing business. There is a great deal of charter shipping to pick up. I handle those businesses from our offices in Athens. Help my father with international oil and freight. Those are his main interests."

A black-and-white photograph shows a smiling young Kyrios flanked by a stern-looking man and woman. The young Kyrios looks like a bright lad, eager to please. His manner stands in stark contrast to the cruelty in his father's eyes.

"My grandparents," Hecate says. "They're gone now. My grandfather had my role at the time that picture was taken. He handled the Aegean businesses while my great-grandfather ran the international."

"Your great-grandfather?"

Hecate steps to the end of the mantel. There, a sepia-toned photograph shows an older man with a brush mustache. Another boy, this time a younger image of Hecate's grandfather. The older man is handsome and stern. The boy exhibits the same cruel features visible in the more recent photograph.

"Where's your great-grandmother?"

"She was killed," Hecate says. The girl's features darken.

"Killed? How?"

"My great-grandfather fled Turkiye in 1920. It was a period when they chased many Orthodox Christians and Jews from the country. The family packed their things into a cart and left. Then, my great-grandmother remembered she had forgotten an icon. She went back to the house to fetch it. My great-grandfather ran back to tell her not to bother. He arrived just in time to see Turkish soldiers drag her from the house. They stood her against a wall. She was clutching the icon to her chest. They shot her—through the icon."

"I'm sorry."

Hecate holds my eyes with hers. "Why? It's not your fault. That is my family's history. My great-grandfather fled to Greece. Worked on fishing boats. Bought an old British tramp freighter with his savings. Paid scrap value. From there, he built his fleet."

"The oil business?"

"Yes, but that is another story." Hecate smiles. "I shall let my father tell you that. All I will say is that he lives in constant fear of being rendered stateless. The stories of my great-grandfather's flight from Turkiye haunt him. Now I think you should go upstairs and unpack."

Kyrios and Harding-James have walked onto the terrace.

Stein's gone upstairs, and Theo stands ready to guide me to my room.

I'm reluctant to leave Hecate. Find myself enthralled by her family's story. She leaves me with Theo and goes to join her father.

My room overlooks the terrace and the ocean. I look down and see Kyrios, Hecate, and Harding-James standing at the rail, looking out to sea. Go to my duffel and lay out a change of clothes on the bed.

At the bottom of the duffel is a box of fifty .45 caliber hollow points and two spare magazines. I take out my Mark 23 and drop the magazine. Rack the slide and watch the extracted round spin onto the bed. I check the mag well, the chamber, and the bolt face. Slap a fresh magazine into the butt and release the slide. Decock the weapon and shove it into my waistband.

I pick up the loose round and open the box of ammo. Top up the half-empty magazine, squeeze it and the other spare into my hip pocket.

My Cold Steel OSS sits in a sheath with Velcro straps. I take it from the duffel, hike my trouser leg, and fasten the sheath to my right calf, upside-down. Tug my pants leg over it. This way, I can draw it from the sheath without impediment.

There's a knock on the door. I push the box of ammo into the duffel and pull the drawstring tight. "Come."

Stein pushes the door open and steps inside. Closes the door behind her.

"The team have put together their report," she says. "Orlov's data has cut our search area by at least three-quarters."

"We still don't know where the *Medusa* is."

"No, but we know where it is *likely* to be hidden."

"Show me."

My room has a small balcony. I close the sliding door so we can't be heard from outside. We sit next to each other at a round coffee table between the bed and the balcony. Stein opens her briefcase and sets her laptop on the table.

She displays a map of Greece. At the bottom are two islands—Crete and Rhodes—the mouth of the Aegean. Between them is a smaller island, Karpathos. An "X" has been marked between Karpathos and Rhodes.

"That 'X' is the first anomaly in *Medusa's* transponder record," Stein says. "All the data indicates that is where she was taken."

"Okay."

"The spoofed transponder readings show her traveling north. We know those are false. The Russian readings from her weather radar show her traveling south-by-west. She skirted the northern coast of Karpathos, then steamed straight for the eastern tip of Crete."

Crete is a large island, and it lies almost directly on a west-to-east line. The northern coast faces the Sea of Crete, part of the Aegean. The southern coast faces the Libyan Sea, part of the Mediterranean.

"Which way did she head from there? North or south?"

"Probably south. The north coast is built up. NATO has Souda Bay Navy Base in the northwest. Heraklio is on the north coast, and so are a ton of beach resorts. The south coast is much more rugged. Inland, the south is less developed. The roads are more like goat trails. Fewer resorts. The beaches are hard to reach."

"What do the satellite photographs show?"

Stein frowns. "I've re-tasked everything we have available

to cover Crete. I've also pulled in the drone I had searching the Cyclades. Now both drones are overflying Crete. So far, nothing."

"I don't get it. ISR is pervasive. On the battlefield, a trooper can't so much as pick his nose without getting droned. How are we missing a six-thousand-ton freighter?"

"It has to be hidden in a cave somewhere."

I shake my head. "It would have to be a monster cave. The *Medusa* is four hundred feet long, sixty feet wide, and a hundred feet from the bottom of her keel to the tops of her masts."

"They could have chopped down her masts."

"Yes, they could. Now that they have the ship and the gold, the ship is disposable. A trivial fifteen million."

"Tomorrow, I'll arrange for a helo to pick you up. You can fly low-level reconnaissance around Crete. Check out the caves on the coast."

"And how will *you* occupy yourself?"

"I'll work the drone and satellite data. We might be missing something."

"Yeah. A six-thousand-ton freighter."

6

THE SECOND DAY – EARLY EVENING, ÉSPEROS

The buzz of conversation and Greek music filters from the terrace. Stein and I descend the stairs to find ourselves in the middle of a party. The mix of guests is unusual. Hecate is twenty-seven. I expected to see a crowd of young people. Instead, most are middle-aged, in suits or dressy casual garb.

Harding-James joins us, drink in hand.

"Not quite the party one expects for a twenty-seven-year-old girl," I say.

"No, it's for the Executive Vice President of Operations for Kyrios Shipping."

A liveried servant holds a silver tray of drinks out to us. Stein and I each accept a glass of wine. I look across the terrace and see Kyrios and Hecate making the rounds of guests. They're at ease, laughing and joking.

"Hecate had a party with her friends in Athens," Harding-James tells us. "This is something of a coming-out party for her. Thanos is grooming her to take over when he retires. It is a giant step. Hecate will be the only chief executive of Kyrios shipping who did not grow up on the ships."

"Kyrios never had a son?"

"Sadly, no. He loves Hecate dearly. She wanted to go into politics. He told her first she had to take over his business. When it is in safe hands, she can live for herself."

"That sounds unreasonable."

"It's not unusual in Mediterranean cultures. The patriarch's word is law in the family. Apart from that requirement, Thanos dotes on Hecate. She's independent and willful, but she respects his wishes."

"Kyrios has an interesting family history."

"Yes." Harding-James tilts his head toward a burly, well-dressed man with a black beard. He's in his late fifties, but radiates strength and vigor. His silk jacket has been carefully tailored to conceal the power in his frame. He's in conversation with Kyrios. "That man is Drakos. His family has an equally interesting history."

"How so?" Stein asks.

"Kyrios and Drakos grew up together. Their grandfathers were contemporaries. The older Kyrios bought old British freighters, saved them from scrap. Used them to run cargoes between the islands. Drakos's grandfather built his wealth smuggling between Greece, Russia, and Turkiye."

"A ship owner and a smuggler."

"A partnership made in heaven," Harding-James says. "Or hell. Kyrios's grandfather built his wealth as he built his fleet. There were whispers that his ships carried Drakos cargoes, but nothing was ever proven."

"Does that continue today?" I ask.

"I don't think so." Harding-James drains his wine. A servant passes, and the Englishman deftly swaps the empty glass for a full one. "It continued for a long time, though. During World War II, Kyrios's grandfather gambled on running oil tankers from North America to Europe. He bought the tankers and registered them under the Panamanian flag."

"A lot of ships sail under that flag today."

"Panamanian regulations were much more lax than those of the United States. During the war, Panama remained neutral. But it would not allow American vessels to sail under its flag. The Americans were not pleased."

"You're going to tell us Kyrios sailed his tankers under the Panamanian flag," Stein says.

"Indeed I am. Kyrios paid hefty bribes to the Panamanian government. Bribes that included a percentage of profits. The Americans were incandescent, and who can blame them? They refused to allow Kyrios tankers to sail under the protection of their convoys. Kyrios lost ships to U-boats, but he made huge profits and bought more. By the end of the war, he had the largest fleet of oil tankers in the world. He ran the tanker fleet and gave the island fleet to his son to manage."

I see the pattern. "That's what Kyrios is doing with Hecate."

"Yes, it is. It has become traditional training to manage the company. He also allows her to manage his football franchise."

"You mean soccer?"

"Yes. Greek shipowners like Kyrios own all the football clubs in Greece. With one phone call, they can have tens of thousands of people on the streets to overthrow a prime minister. Remember Hecate's interest in politics."

Hecate joins her father and Drakos. The big man takes her hand and kisses her on both cheeks.

"When Kyrios's grandfather retired, he handed the business to his son. Kyrios's father, it is said, took steps to make the Kyrios fleet completely legitimate. He distanced the business from the Drakos trade."

"Is Drakos really a smuggler?"

"So it is whispered. The family runs a trading company. All manner of goods. Grain, wheat, oil, refined petroleum products. Whatever people buy and sell. Over the decades, there has been talk of guns and drugs."

"Colorful bunch."

Stein looks at me sharply.

"It's alright." Harding-James laughs. "Kyrios and Hecate know their family history, they know all the stories, and they know the truth. They could not run their business otherwise. The two families remain friendly. I will tell you one more story."

"So far, the Kyrios story would make great bedtime reading," Stein says. She's flushed, and it's not just the wine.

The islands. The sun. The romance.

"I will tell you this," Harding-James says, "and you can decide. There have been two attempts to kidnap Hecate. Both failed. The first time, she was lucky. The kidnappers were incompetent. One was killed by the police, the other escaped. A week later, he was found on the docks of Kavala. He was hanging from the boom of a freighter. A thin wire had been looped around his neck. His hands and feet were not bound, so it took him a long time to die."

"Did Kyrios do it?" I ask.

Harding-James shrugs. "It doesn't matter. There was

endless speculation. If Kyrios did not have it done, the man was executed by the Drakos family."

"What about the second attempt?"

"Kyrios engaged bodyguards to protect Hecate. They repelled the second attempt. The kidnappers didn't have a chance. Hecate chafes under the constant presence of her bodyguards, but she recognizes their value."

"Didn't look like it today."

"Kyrios worries about his daughter. But a bloodless child is no good to him."

I'll say. Hecate is anything but bloodless.

Kyrios and Drakos approach us. "Ash, you are telling our guests stories, yes? Of our beautiful islands. The sun, the sea. Stories of... love?"

Harding-James laughs. "The Aegean is full of stories," he says. "Of love, and battles. Kings and heroes. The rise and fall of empires."

"Since Helen's face launched a thousand ships, yes?"

"Yes. Since Achilles fought Paris. Since Leonidas held the pass at Thermopylae."

"Come," Kyrios says. "Let me introduce you to my friend, Drakos. Our families have known each other for generations."

Drakos's hand is like that of Kyrios. Callused, and backed by a powerful grip. He might be wearing a five-thousand-dollar suit, but he's spent a lifetime at physical labor.

"Our families have run parallel courses," Drakos says. "But Thanos is of the sea. My family are humble merchants who buy and sell goods."

"Ah, you are too modest." Kyrios claps Drakos on the back. "Without your business, my ships would have nothing to fill their bellies."

Hecate joins us. "Why don't we have supper?"

"Of course, of course," Kyrios says. "Let us dine together."

There are rectangular tables arranged around the periphery of the terrace. The band occupies one corner near the entrance to the living room. A number of circular tables have been arranged in an arc next to a space cleared for dancing.

Kyrios gallantly pulls a chair for Stein, and the Deputy Director accepts the gesture graciously. Our host and I seat ourselves on either side of her. Hecate sits between her father and Drakos, and the bearded man sits on my right.

The sun is setting, the sky and sea are ablaze on the horizon. The white of Kyrios's yacht, the *Grigoro Fidi*, glows pale orange. The waters to our right darken to midnight blue. Soon, as dusk descends, the water will go black.

I look up and notice the sky is changing color. Blood red to the west, dark blue to the east. This sunset will not last long. I lean back to enjoy it, allow the conversation to wash over me. High to the east, a bright light arcs across the sky. A shooting star, or a satellite?

If it's a satellite, the *Grigoro Fidi* will show up clearly on its imagery. At the right angle, one will be able to read the name painted on her bow and stern. Is the satellite ours, or is it Russian? Whoever is operating it, they'll be able to count the number of guests on the terrace, read the license plates of the cars parked inside the wall.

Did the pirates *really* mutilate the *Medusa* and steam her into a cave? They must have. We've defined a conservative search radius. Blanketed the area with satellite and drone coverage. Found nothing.

How else could they evade our all-seeing eyes?

7

THE SECOND DAY – EVENING, GRIGORO FIDI

K yrios serves a fine dinner of endless dishes. Greek salad, skewers of chicken and lamb souvlaki, tzatziki, and a procession of seafood specialties. Like the wine, the seafood has been provided by local fishermen.

The old man and Hecate are perfect hosts, introducing us to different dishes. There's a parade of *saganaki*—seafood appetizers. Shrimp and cheese *saganaki*—fresh shrimp deglazed in ouzo, covered in tomato sauce and feta cheese. Served in a big frying pan carried by two metal handles.

Baked fish, *psari plaki,* is served on plates of Greek lemon rice. The plates of mussels are endless.

After the second course, Hecate excuses herself and moves from table to table. She greets her guests and ensures they are enjoying their meals. For all his gruff appearance, Drakos plays his part, explaining how dishes are prepared.

Kyrios passes around two massive platters of lobster pasta. He has us pass both ways. It's not a western lobster pasta, with small shreds of lobster meat mixed up with spaghetti. Kyrios's lobster pasta consists of whole lobsters, sectioned and prepared with care, set on beds of spaghetti.

The band performs Greek folk music. They play stringed instruments, from lutes to guitars. They play drums and, on occasion, tambourines. Two women and a man take turns singing.

"This song is so sad," Stein says, "but it has a sense of... valor."

"Ah," Drakos says. "I am pleased you have detected that. This is klephtic. A little modernized perhaps, but it dates from the time of the Greek revolution. When we fought the Turks for independence. Our most heroic people fled to the mountains and fought the Ottomans from there. These are songs of love, exile, and rebellion."

Kyrios leans forward. "Greeks often quarrel, but they unite against an oppressor. This, I love about these people. These islands. My family is from Turkiye, you know this? My grandfather was forced to leave in 1920. From then on, we became Greek."

"Your family was exiled?" Stein asks.

"Yes. Many Jews and Orthodox Christians were forced to leave."

"My family was forced from the Soviet Union about the same time yours left Turkiye," Stein says.

"Ah." Kyrios leans forward and puts his hand on Stein's arm. "You are Jewish?"

"Yes," Stein says. "My family were Lithuanian Jews. They moved to the United States long ago. It's been good to us."

Kyrios leans back and claps his hands. "Yes. The United States. Land of the free, yes? Let us drink to our American friends. And the English. My dear, dear friend, Ash. Your great Lord Byron died in Missolonghi, fighting for our independence. He was only thirty-eight years old."

We raise our glasses and toast America and Great Britain. The heroes of Greece—from those who fought alongside Lord Byron, to Achilles, to King Leonidas. Kyrios is an enthralling character and the wine is flowing.

Night has fallen. The *Grigoro Fidi* is a cluster of lights floating on a black ocean. The sky is a vast field of stars. I look for shooting stars.

Or satellites.

"You are fascinated by my boat, Breed." Kyrios leans back and lights up a cigarette.

"It is a beautiful ship."

"The *Grigoro Fidi*," Kyrios says proudly. "It is not the biggest super-yacht in those harbors we visit. But it is beautiful for what I designed it to do."

"You designed it?" Stein sounds taken aback.

"I did." Kyrios laughs. "Dear Anya, I am a peasant. But I know what I want, and I know what I do not know. I hired the best engineers, the best naval architects. Told them what I wanted. Had them build it. Spared no expense."

Impressed, Stein says nothing.

"Come." Kyrios slaps his knee. "I will give you a tour of the *Fidi*."

"Right now, Thanos?" Drakos is surprised.

"Of course. We will be gone but an hour." Kyrios takes a mobile phone from his pocket. Punches a speed dial, gives instructions. "Let us go. The whaleboat awaits."

Kyrios leads us off the terrace. Stone steps wind from the clifftop to the beach below. The steps are lit by ropes of colored lights strung on metal safety rails.

"Do not tell her." Kyrios laughs. "One day, Hecate will

marry. I will arrange the ceremony on the beach. We will erect gazebos. On a warm summer night, the procession will descend these steps. Lighted just so."

"Isn't he amazing?" Stein clutches my arm with one hand. She's holding a half-full wine glass in the other. The CIA's Deputy Director of Special Situations is getting squiffed.

In minutes, we're on the beach. There's a boathouse to the right, and a short pier. The pier is bathed in the warm glow of sodium lights. A blue-and-white whaleboat bobs in the water. Two sailors in spotless white uniforms are in the boat. One at the prow, one at the stern. The man at the stern manages the outboard.

Kyrios shouts something in Greek. The sailor at the prow throws us a rope. Water from the wet hemp splashes my face, and I get a taste of salty Mediterranean water. Kyrios catches the rope with the skill of a man who's spent a lifetime at sea.

"Careful. Be careful."

Drakos has no problem getting into the boat. Stein, tipsy as she is, manages to keep her balance. Kyrios, Drakos, and I have to help Harding-James into the boat. For a moment, he has one leg in the boat and one trailing on the pier. I fear we're going to lose him, but Drakos yanks on the Englishman's arm and hauls him in.

Harding-James makes good money insuring maritime cargoes, but he obviously spends no time at sea.

The sailor extends his hand. I'm not too proud to take it, and in seconds I'm aboard. Kyrios follows me.

The old man instructs us where to sit. His practiced eye trims the whaleboat. The sailor at the stern starts the outboard, and in minutes we are forging our way to the

Grigoro Fidi. I look back at Ésperos. The big house is lighted and the strains of music carry to us over the water.

In minutes, we're tied up next to the *Fidi.* No boarding ladder here. The crew, all dressed in white uniforms, some with blue-and-white striped T-shirts, lower a boarding gangway. It's a metal staircase that folds flush to the deck but can be lowered for passengers. The metal steps are covered with a synthetic non-slip material with the texture of sandpaper. It's easy to climb to the well deck.

"Now I will show you my pride and joy." Kyrios touches Stein's arm with his right hand, gestures expansively with his left. "I *imagined* it. And it is here. There is nothing more exciting than to make an idea come alive, yes?"

The *Grigoro Fidi* is sleek and bigger than I thought. All of a hundred tons and one-hundred-and-twenty feet long. Two flags wave at the fantail. The flag of Greece, and the flag of Kyrios Shipping. Looking forward, we admire the *Grigoro Fidi*'s graceful length.

"You are standing over her engines," Kyrios says. "Four screws, four gas turbines. Powerful enough to drive her at fifty knots. There is not a man'o'war afloat that can catch her. We carry enough fuel for an operating radius of four hundred miles."

He's not kidding. Given her dimensions and performance, the *Fidi* could serve as the prototype for a class of high-performance missile patrol boats.

"How hot do those engines run?" I ask.

"One thousand degrees Celsius," Kyrios says. "You see the funnels—to ventilate and cool them. I know what you are thinking, Breed. Any aircraft or satellite with thermal imaging will have no difficulty finding the *Fidi*. But we rarely operate on four screws, and we have backup supercharged diesels as well."

"*When* do you operate on four screws?"

Kyrios laughs. "When I choose to indulge my fancy." The after well deck has been laid out with a table, deck chairs, and glasses of wine. Kyrios gestures for us to help ourselves. Glass in hand, he leads us forward. Companionways lead up to a boat deck and the navigation bridge. Kyrios points them out, but leads us straight ahead into the saloon. It's wide and spacious, with soft carpet, leather armchairs, sofas, and a well-stocked bar. Against one wall is a map of the world, on a massive digital display. The kind they have in Times Square.

"There is nowhere in the world the *Fidi* cannot go," Kyrios says. "Provided there is ocean."

The old man smiles, sips his wine, stares at the map. "Ésperos is my home," he says to himself. "But if I am ever forced to leave, I have many homes."

"Why would you leave?" Stein asks.

"Why would anyone leave? Why did my family leave Turkiye? Why did yours leave Lithuania? A man's duty is to his family. To care for them, provide for them, protect them. It is my duty to worry. Anya, it is my duty to think of everything."

Kyrios turns to me. "It would not be hard to find the *Fidi*, Breed. But it will be hard to take her."

The old man touches a button and the map of the world slides to one side. Behind it is a shocking arsenal. In a concealed case set in the bulkhead are racks of M14 sniper rifles, M4 carbines, and SIG P226 pistols. My eyes are drawn to a deep recess in the bulkhead. Olive drab tubes have been stacked in a special rack.

"My God. Are those..."

Kyrios laughs. "Javelins and Stingers, Breed. Repackaged to fit on board. The *Fidi* has anti-air and anti-ship capability."

A shelf above the missile tubes holds CLUs—Command Launch Units—for Javelin anti-tank missiles. Next to them are packed IFF antennae assemblies and Battery Cooling Units for Stinger anti-aircraft missiles. These are extremely sophisticated weapons.

"Where did you get them?"

Kyrios laughs. "Breed, you are not a naïve man. Your wars in Ukraine and Afghanistan have scattered these weapons far and wide. The soldiers you give them to cannot wait to sell them for the price of a passport."

"It takes training to use these."

"Of course. My men have been trained by former American Special Forces and British Special Boat Service. The *Fidi*'s captain and mates are former officers of the Kriegsmarine."

Kyrios touches the button a second time and the panel slides shut. "You know, the biggest problem I have with your weapons is ensuring that they work. The cooling units have a limited shelf life and must be replaced. My suppliers sell me more BCUs than they do missiles."

I stare at the tycoon. It's clear he understands the nuances of the weapons, if only from a practical perspective. The Battery Cooling Units contain argon gas, which leaks from the housing. The actual shelf life of a BCU varies with conditions, but I'd change them out every six months. Ex-Special Forces contractors in his employ must have informed him of the problem.

Kyrios raises his arms to the sky. "What am I to do? I

tried to find British missiles, but they have none left. I shall
have to find Russian or Swedish missiles somewhere, yes?
Maybe Egyptians or Turks will sell them to me. Ah... but I
do not like the Turks."

The old man laughs, claps me on the shoulder.

A companionway leads below. "Those are the living
quarters," Kyrios says. "My family and guests sleep
forward, the crew aft. Hecate and I have private cabins, and
there are two more that accommodate two guests each. We
shall not visit those compartments today. Forward of the
saloon, and beneath the navigation bridge, is the pilot
house. It is here that we maneuver, navigate and
communicate."

The pilot house is impressive. There is a chair for the
captain, another for the helmsman, and a third to the right
of the helmsman. The helmsman's station is arranged more
like the controls of an airplane than a ship. The man sits in a
comfortable bucket seat with lap and shoulder harness.
That alone suggests the *Fidi* is capable of hard maneuvering.
The traditional helm has been replaced by a control yoke
similar to those found on Boeing airliners. The man's right
hand naturally falls on the throttles of four gas turbine
engines.

To the helmsman's right is another bucket seat, currently
unoccupied. On the control panel between that seat and the
helmsman are the *Fidi*'s radios. In front of the second seat,
but arranged so that they are visible to the helmsman, are
radar displays, GPS, AIS, and other navigation equipment.

"Under normal conditions," Kyrios says, "there are five
bridge crew. Captain, helmsman, radio operator, and two
lookouts. The radio operator also manages the radar and
depth sounder. Right now, the lookouts are above us on the

navigation bridge, and we can make do without the radio operator."

A narrow companionway leads to the navigation bridge. "There is not much to see there," Kyrios says. "If we climbed, we would have to put down our drinks. Come, let us finish them in the saloon, then return to the party."

We return to the saloon and sink into leather seats as soft as butter. Kyrios and Drakos engage in light conversation with Stein and Harding-James.

My mind drifts to another cabinet with its own racks of weapons. The cabinet on the *Goliath*, with its G3s, MP5s, and USPs. And hand grenades. The nature of the weapons was similar to those aboard the *Fidi*. Long rifles with sufficient range to be effective at sea. Carbines and submachine guns for close quarters combat. Sidearms.

Similar weapons, but acquired from different sources. The pirate crew bought German equipment. Kyrios has purchased American rifles and Swiss handguns.

Perhaps there are such things as coincidences.

8

THE SECOND DAY – LATE EVENING, ÉSPEROS

The party is in full swing by the time we get back to Ésperos. Many guests have changed tables to mix and mingle. The music is lively and couples have taken to the dance floor. There are cries of *Hopa!* I don't speak Greek, but it's easy enough to figure out. *Hopa* must be a Greek version of *Hoo-rah!*

I collapse into my chair next to Harding-James. The Englishman is gasping from the climb. I'm breathing hard, but recovering quickly. As usual, Stein is unaffected by exercise. If anything, she seems energized.

Stein turns to me. "Come on, Breed. Let's dance."

The Deputy Director is glowing. Her cheeks are flushed from the wine. This is *not* a good idea. "I'm resting up, Stein. Tomorrow's going to be a busy day."

"Dance?" Kyrios brightens, straightens in his chair. "You want to dance? Anya, I will dance with you."

Stein demurs. "Thanos, I'm trying to show Breed how to *live* a little. I want to know if this machine has a *heart*."

What the fuck. This is new.

There's a loud crash from the dance floor. I jerk and my hand goes to the butt of the Mark 23.

Hopa!

Someone's thrown a plate onto the tiled floor.

Annoyed, I relax. Loosen the knots in my shoulders.

A voluptuous brunette steps onto the dance floor. Alone, she raises her arms and spreads them on either side. Sways to the music. Her body's all curves, like a Greek goddess, a sculpture come to life. She's a sinuous symphony, hips tilting, legs crossing and uncrossing. With each step, her ankles turn just so.

The woman loiters at our table, dances in front of Kyrios. Her eyes flash, meet the old man's. He stares at her, and he's not old, never has been. He gets up and spreads his arms to mirror her stance.

Hopa! Hopa!

Guests clap and smash more plates on the floor. The air is filled with music and the sound of crashing dishes. Across the room, Hecate beams. Picks up a plate and throws it. The other couples on the floor melt to the sidelines to watch Kyrios and the woman dance.

Across the table from me, Drakos leans back in his chair. He's been pounding down the ouzo, and he tips back another glass. "*Yasou,*" he says. His eyes follow Kyrios and the woman. "*Yasou.*"

Stein twists around to watch.

Kyrios and the woman dance around each other. They're touching, but not. The woman leans back against him, arms spread. They're a hairsbreadth apart. He spreads his arms to hers. His fingers touch the backs of her hands, feather-light. She tilts her head back, close enough for him to catch the scent of her hair, the nape of her neck. The dance is a sensuous seduction.

The music quickens, and the dancers break apart. Kyrios and the woman clap in time and dance around each other. It's an exuberant display of yin and yang, masculinity and femininity.

Hopa!

More plates crash. The guests clap in unison. Caught up in the gaiety, Stein joins in the clapping.

Kyrios and the woman whirl like dervishes. Kyrios yells with exuberance. "*Hopa!*"

The music slows. It stops, and immediately resumes with a slow, sensuous rhythm. The woman throws her arms around Kyrios and hugs him. Crushes her ample bosom to his chest, grabs his back and shoulders.

Kyrios is happy to be engulfed. With a beatific smile, he hugs the woman back.

Stein stiffens, straightens in her chair.

The woman tilts her face to Kyrios, strokes his cheek with her palm.

Hopa! Hopa!

"*Yasou*," Drakos says.

"Fuck this." Stein reaches up and undoes her hair. It falls about her shoulders in a black waterfall.

What's she doing?

Stein stands up, tears off her suit jacket, throws it on a chair. Grabs a plate and throws it on the tiles.

"*Hopa!*" Hecate yells.

I'm too late to drag Stein off the floor. "For God's sake. Stein, sit *down*."

Stein raises her arms and advances on Kyrios. The band plays, the music slow and sensuous. Holstered pistol in full view, the Deputy Director's hips sway. The guests don't mind. They're used to seeing weapons around the Kyrios estate.

"*Yasou*," Drakos says again. The big guy's sinking into an ouzo-soaked daze. He looks at me as though channeling great wisdom. "My friend, there is *one* sin for which there is no absolution."

"Bet you a nickel you're going to tell me."

"When a woman wants you to take her to bed, you *must* go. It is your *duty*."

I scowl. Not sure I need this much wisdom from a Greek smuggler.

"God *may* forgive," Drakos says, "but *she* will not."

Kyrios turns to Stein. Smoldering, her eyes fix on his.

Reluctantly, the Greek woman allows Stein to cut in. Kyrios and Stein sway toward each other, moving to the music. I don't know where Stein learned to dance, but she looks amazing.

The pace of the music quickens. Kyrios and Stein whirl around each other. Hecate and the guests clap with delight. Stein's hair flies about her head, obscures her face.

And the music slows. Kyrios spreads his arms and Stein leans back against him. She moves the way the Greek woman did, only... better. I've never seen her like this. The Harvard nerd is gone, replaced by a siren. Kyrios brushes her fingers, closes his eyes, intoxicated.

"*Yasou*." Drakos's eyelids are heavy. He's out of it.

"Breed, I will teach you to dance."

A woman's voice. Rosy-cheeked and smiling, Hecate stands over me.

"No, thank you."

Hecate takes me by the hand and pulls me to my feet. "I insist."

Reluctant, I allow the girl to guide me. I'm conscious Hecate is playing wing girl to her father. What a pair *they* make.

"This is a kind of *syrtaki*," Hecate says. "A bit modern. Let us do it together."

She stands next to me, facing away from the dance floor. Raises her arms and puts a hand on my shoulder. "Come on, put your hand on *my* shoulder. I don't bite."

I do as she says, find that our arms naturally touch. The sensation is electric.

"Follow me," Hecate says. "Kick. And back."

Hecate laughs. "Good. Again."

It's not hard. Hecate takes a knee and I follow her example. We spring upright together. "Not bad," she says. "Breed, you have potential."

The pace quickens and Hecate shows me her steps. Now it's hard. I am *not* a born dancer. I give up trying to follow her, start dancing on my own. Get out of my head, just give it. The guests are clapping and throwing plates.

Hooooooopa!

Hecate stops, breathless. I find myself still dancing.

"Enough!" Hecate puts her hands on my shoulders, draws me aside. "Breed, you're crazy. Let's rest."

The band plays a new piece, and guests return to the dance floor. Hecate leans on me, lays her face against my chest. My eyes search the terrace. Kyrios and Stein are gone.

Hecate runs her fingers through my hair. Hand flat against the back of my head, she pulls gently. It's a delicious feeling. She lifts her face to me, and we kiss.

"Come on." Hecate takes me by the hand and leads me from the terrace.

The band plays on.

HECATE LEADS me through the living room and up the stairs. Guests are everywhere, but I feel like we're invisible. She lets me into her room, shuts the door behind us. The lights are dim. It's a girl's room. Only a girl would devote attention to colored bedspreads. Matching pillow covers. Matching carpet. She stands with her back to the door, hands flat on the wood. Stares at me, cheeks flushed, lips moist.

My heart pounds in my chest. We're giving in to the attraction we felt from the moment we met at the hotel.

From low in her throat, Hecate moans. Clutches me. We kiss and bite, fall onto the floor. She mounts me, fights for leverage. My hands go under her skirt, find her underwear. I tear away the light material and cast it aside. She reaches down, fingers grasping, and pulls me into her.

We thrash together on the carpet. Hecate opens my shirt and pulls the Mark 23 from my waistband. She glances at the weapon and tosses it aside. Decocked and drop-safe, it lands with a clunk. Does she know it's drop-safe? We shed clothes, thrash some more. Laughing, she says something about her knees. I lift her up, enjoy the sensation of testing my muscles against her weight. Throw her naked onto the bed. She's still laughing. Raises herself on her elbows.

"Take me," she says.

9

THE THIRD DAY – MORNING, ÉSPEROS

When I wake up, Hecate is gone. I check my watch. It's nine o'clock, and the sun's up. I swear and swing myself off the bed. Snatch my clothes off the floor and get dressed.

I slide the magazine out of the Mark 23. It's heavy, full of .45 caliber hollow points. I slap it back into the grip and make sure it's seated in the mag well. Do a press check, slide it behind my belt. Tug my shirt down.

Rush downstairs. Servants are cleaning up the living room and terrace. What a devastated piece of territory. Stein is sitting at a table, nibbling a croissant. Checking emails on her laptop. She finished her morning run long ago.

She doesn't bother to look up. "Good morning, Breed. Tough night robbing the cradle?"

Where is *this* coming from? "Get off my back, Stein. Who told *you* to fuck the host?"

Stein shoots to her feet. "Who I fuck is none of your business!"

We stare at each other. Stein opens her clenched fists.

The irony isn't lost on her. More years separate her from Kyrios than separate me from Hecate.

I need air. Brush past Stein, step to the terrace.

"The USS *Pressley Bannon* is tied up at Souda Bay Navy Base in Crete." Stein stares at me over her shoulder. "A Sea Hawk will pick you up at eleven o'clock."

"Captain Cruik feeling generous?"

"It's Rear Admiral Cruik now. The *Pressley Bannon* is captained by Commander Katie Palomas. I went through the Secretary of the Navy. SECNAV green-lighted Sixth Fleet to provide resources."

Stein's access amazes me. She has powerful patrons in the Company. Her family's wealth and her father's connections open doors. Enough to get the Secretary of the Navy to take a Deputy Director's phone call.

"What will *you* be doing?"

"I'll work the data. All our air and space assets are drawing blanks. Ditto the signals intelligence. It looks like the *Medusa*'s gone to ground."

The fight's gone out of us, but the tension hasn't gone away. The outburst surfaced something we've recognized but never dealt with.

"Palomas is a good officer," I say. "I'll be ready."

"That Huey is still on the pad. The Sea Hawk will set down on the beach under those bluffs to the west."

I turn and walk onto the terrace. Servants are sweeping up the broken crockery. Hecate is reclining on a deck chair, reading a book.

"Have you been married long?" The girl's smile is mischievous.

I stand at the rail next to her. Stare at the peaceful beach scene. The blue water, the cloudless sky, the *Grigoro Fidi* moored a hundred and fifty yards offshore. "Don't *you* start."

One night together and it feels like we've been friends for years. I don't even mind she played her father's wing girl.

Hecate closes her book and sits on the edge of the deck chair. She's wearing a faded Cambridge T-shirt and matte fuchsia-colored shorts. Her feet are bare. I detect faint traces of carpet burn on her knees. I smile.

She catches me looking and blushes. "It was fun."

"Yes, it was."

"Want to go for a walk on the beach?"

"Sure."

Hecate's careful not to step on the broken dishes. Together, we descend the stone stairs.

"Do you really want to run your father's company?"

"I don't have a choice. It's my duty."

"You have a right to live your own life."

Hecate shrugs. "That's a very American attitude. Here, we feel differently. Besides, it's fun and it's not inconsistent with what I want to do."

"What do you want to do?"

"Become President of Greece."

For a moment I want to ask if she's serious, but I can tell she'd be insulted. "Why?"

"I don't think our leaders serve the people. I can do better."

I'm sure she can.

"Where's your father this morning?"

"He's playing golf with Mr Harding-James and Drakos. They decided to let you sleep."

"How well do you know Drakos?"

"I know our family histories. Does that mean I know

him? I always feel there are doors in his house that must not
be opened."

"Do you know everything about your father?"

"Everything I need to know," Hecate says. "I know my
family distanced themselves from certain activities of the
Drakos family. I know they remained close. That is not
unusual in Greece. We do not tear up a relationship that has
lasted four generations."

"Does Drakos still engage in illegal activities?"

"I am sure he does. So long as they do not interfere with
my family business, I don't concern myself."

"That man who tried to kidnap you?"

Hecate stops and stares at me. "You heard the stories. I
was fifteen."

"Young."

"He didn't touch me. I am sure it was Drakos's men who
killed him. The police investigated all my father's people."

"Your families *are* close."

"There are reasons to *not* tear up generations-old rela-
tionships."

We walk and talk. At the end of the beach, we sit on a
piece of driftwood. "That tattoo on your arm," Hecate says.

They always ask this. "What about it?"

"Why is the flag backward? With the stars on the right
side?"

"In the old days, wars were fought by long ranks of men
who charged and tried to kill each other. The man bearing
the flag led the way. In the wind, the flag would blow it backward. Viewed from the right, the field of stars appeared that
way. If the flag bearer was shot, another man would grab the
flag and continue on."

"Is that what you are about, Breed? Gallantry?"

"There's nothing gallant about getting shot in the face. I care about winning. That's not always consistent with gallant behavior."

"You're like my father."

"How so?"

"He taught me that business is war. He taught me to do business with a loaded gun in my pocket."

"Sounds like good advice."

"Like my father, you care about doing the right thing."

My survival radio buzzes. It's Stein. "Yes?"

"Your helo will be here in five minutes," Stein says. The Deputy Director sounds testy. She's probably watching us right now.

"Roger that."

I disconnect the call and squeeze the radio back in my pocket. Get to my feet. "There she is."

The Sea Hawk appears, a speck in the distance. It grows in size until it hovers over the beach. The roar of its rotor assaults our ears.

I take Hecate's arm and we step back thirty yards. The rotor wash blasts the surf and scatters sand in all directions.

The helo is a modern MH-60R Sea Hawk, configured for anti-submarine warfare and surface interdiction. There's a FLIR—forward looking infrared—pod on its nose, equipped with a laser designator. Electronic Support Measure sensors are mounted on either side, and a data link antenna has been tucked under the helo's chin. A magnetic anomaly detector has been mounted in the tail.

The Sea Hawk is not carrying missiles or air-launched torpedoes. Today, the helo's not quite a flying gas can, but it's flying light to extend its search range.

The pilot sets the helo down on the beach and cuts

power. It looks like a big insect with its powerful main rotor and reverse tricycle landing gear—two wheels forward, one aft. The word NAVY is stenciled in large blue letters on the boom. The pilots are visible through the windscreens in the cockpit. The flight engineer stands in the cargo door.

I give Hecate a chaste hug. "I'll see you this afternoon."

"Good luck."

"We're still looking for the right haystack," I say.

Hecate smiles. "You'll find your haystack, Breed. The needle, too."

I stride toward the Sea Hawk.

"Breed."

I turn. Hecate thrusts her hands into the pockets of her shorts. "Stein likes you."

"How do *you* know?"

"Women *always* know. But you know it too."

Shake my head, jog to the helo. I need to stay focused.

The flight engineer lends me a hand and I boost myself into the compartment. There's a jump seat for the flight engineer behind the two pilots. Four seats occupy the center of the bay, facing out toward the sliding doors. The portside door is closed, the starboard door is open.

I notice that the design and arrangement of the seats is unusual. The flight engineer's jump seat is plain enough, but the other four seats look like they were built for a carnival ride. The seats are attached to H-frames with supports that reach almost to the overhead. The seats are attached to the horizontal bars of the Hs, adjustable for height.

Miniguns on articulated mounts are stowed next to both doors. If necessary, they can be swung out and operated by the men seated in the gunner seats. A hydraulic rescue hoist is mounted above the starboard door where it can be operated by the flight engineer. Extendable fast rope bars are fixed to the overhead. When extended with cables attached, they can be used to quickly land boarding parties or special operations troops.

"I'm Keller," the flight engineer says. He gestures to another man sitting in the aft gunner seat, port side. "The nerd with all the games is Reznick. He's our ASW—Anti-submarine Warfare—technician."

The pilots have wound down the engines to a low rumble. It's unusual to be able to converse in a helo without using an intercom.

Reznick lifts a hand in greeting. He sits behind a metal desk. It's stacked with electronic equipment, charts, and a laptop. "This is our anti-submarine warfare suite," he says.

The pilot climbs out of his seat and joins us in the cargo compartment. Shakes my hand. "I'm Lieutenant Commander Ellison," he says. "Copilot over there is Lieutenant Carlyle. Commander Palomas briefed us on the broad requirements of your mission. We need to talk specifics."

"We've narrowed the search area to the eastern tip of Crete and the south coast," I tell him. "We're looking for a six-thousand-ton freighter. Four hundred feet long, sixty feet wide. It's a hundred feet high, but the hijackers would not be shy about lopping off the masts."

"Did our satellites and drones pick up anything?" Ellison asks.

"Nothing. We've learned this much from signals intelligence."

"If satellites and drones didn't spot it, the ship has to be in a cave."

"There are a lot of caves along that coast," Reznick says.

"Some are wide and deep. Not many are a hundred feet high."

"How many are sixty feet high?"

"I can only think of three."

"You guys know this area?"

"Some," Ellison says. "We definitely spend more time around the north coast."

Reznick opens a chart on the table. "Why don't you show us your best guess, Mr Breed?"

I squint at the chart. "We want the southeast coast of the Lasithi region. This crescent extending from Ierapetra to just east of Sitia. Any islands in the vicinity big enough to hide the *Medusa*."

"What do you think?" Ellison asks Reznick.

"A hundred miles, tops. We can cover it."

I exchange glances with Ellison. "Crank 'er up and let's get airborne."

Ellison feeds power to the Sea Hawk's twin engines. The rotor spins up and the pilot hauls on the collective. With a shudder, the helo lifts off. I strap myself in and look out the door. Hecate stands on the beach, waving. I wave back.

The helo turns, tips slightly nose-down, and picks up speed.

Destination Crete.

10

THE THIRD DAY – LATE MORNING, CRETE

The Sea Hawk makes its way west toward Crete. Keller sits in the flight engineer's jump seat. I occupy the starboard gunner seat with my back to Reznick. I'm wearing Nikon binoculars around my neck. The binoculars are black, with US NAVY stamped in white letters on the metal frame. At my feet is an international orange flare pistol and a box of flares.

We see oil tankers and container ships plying the waves. The Mediterranean to our left, the Aegean to the right. These vessels are many times the size of *Medusa* and *Goliath*. In places, we see fishing trawlers. Singly and in groups.

"We'll fly a systematic pattern," Ellison says. The thunder of the rotors makes communication by intercom a necessity. "We'll work our way from east to west. Reznick's marked the caves we know about, but we'll check out anything else that makes sense."

Ellison has his own binoculars. While Carlyle flies the Sea Hawk, Ellison and I scan the beaches and cliffs.

"Take her down, Greg," Ellison tells Carlyle.

The copilot takes the helo down to a hundred feet and throttles back to thirty-five knots. We begin a slow and painstaking search from two hundred yards off the coast.

"The sun is shining from overhead," Ellison says. "We have to pay attention to outcrops and overhangs. They conceal caves in shadow."

He's right. The sun, the Aegean, and the romance are wonderful. But at this moment, I'd prefer the diffuse light of an overcast. To fill in the shadows. The craggy cliff faces cast black daggers that make for natural camouflage.

"There's no point crawling over flat beach," I tell him. "We can pick up the pace. Slow down when we go by the cliffs."

The south coast is rugged country. I didn't think it would be this bad. The interior is rocky and mountainous. Devoid of developed roads. The single lanes I've seen are little more than goat trails. There are a few villages, but they're isolated.

I focus the binoculars on the steep, narrow streets of a village. People ride sure-footed donkeys over rough trails that pass for streets. "Picturesque, isn't it? Can't believe people live here."

"A fair bit of the south is unspoiled. I did some hiking by Ierapetra," Ellison says. "There's a reason there aren't a lot of holiday resorts. To get to the beach, you have to either hike or ride a donkey."

Keller laughs. "Imagine honeymooners getting to their hotels smelling like burro."

Inspiration strikes. "Imagine getting intimate with burros," Reznick says.

"Belay that," Ellison says. "We're coming up on the first big cave. Should be over there at two o'clock."

The copilot slows the Sea Hawk to a crawl. I swing the

Nikon to cover the cliff. The face is two hundred feet high, with jagged shadows slashing down to the water. The ocean is a dazzling blue. I see nothing.

"Shit."

I lower the binoculars. Use my sleeve to rub sweat away. Blink, raise the eyepieces back to my eyes.

"It's there," Ellison says. "At three o'clock now. Greg, let's hover."

The copilot hovers two hundred yards from the cliff face.

"Close it up gently." Ellison looks back at me. "See it?"

I see it. The cave mouth is semi-circular. Its black maw blends with the shadows cast by an overhang. It would be easier to spot in the early morning or late afternoon, but here we are.

"I reckon that cave's a bit under a hundred feet," Ellison says. "Tight fit, but you might get your freighter inside. Especially if you lop off her masts."

I strain to see into the cave. "How far into the cliff do you think it extends?"

"No idea. Only way to tell is to come back with a Zodiac and go inside."

"Can you get us closer?"

"My aircraft," Ellison says.

"Your controls." The copilot surrenders control of the Sea Hawk.

Ellison tests the controls. The cyclic, the pedals. "This close to cliffs, you have to watch out for turbulence," he says. "I think we're okay."

The Sea Hawk creeps closer to the cave. I take the flare pistol, break it, and load a magnesium flare. I take careful aim, allow for the trajectory of the flare, and fire it into the cave. The charge bursts into a blazing white sun.

Empty. The cave's mouth is a hundred feet, top to bottom. High enough to accommodate the *Medusa,* masts and all. But the rock walls have collapsed into the gullet of the cavern. The mouth of the opening might be eighty feet wide, but the interior can't be more than fifty.

The pirates could chop off the *Medusa*'s masts and the ship still wouldn't fit.

I swallow my disappointment. "The other two caves you had in mind... Are they this big?"

Ellison shrugs. "One is a bit smaller. The other is bigger, but not much."

"Let's go," I tell him. "Can't fault our methodology. Let's stick to it."

"Your aircraft," Ellison says.

"My controls," Carlyle responds. The Sea Hawk peels away from the cave mouth and we resume our search.

We continue to prowl the south coast. The aircrew point out another large cave. It'll make a great tourist attraction, but it isn't big enough for a dismasted *Medusa*. I nod to Ellison, and he signals Carlyle to keep flying.

We creep along at thirty knots, searching the coast. Out of the corner of my eye, I see a majestic peak that towers above the surrounding three-hundred-foot cliffs. I blink my tired eyes.

"My God, that's a sight." I lower my binoculars and stare at a magnificent structure. Half a mile away, it's perched atop a four-hundred-foot promontory. "Is it a castle?"

Ellison grins. "I didn't warn you because I wanted to see your reaction. It's a Greek Orthodox monastery. Hundreds of years old. The Koitída Sofias—the Cradle of Wisdom. Years ago, the monastic order occupied it and accepted visitors. Those brave enough to venture out here. It's privately owned now. The order couldn't afford its upkeep and decided to sell."

The cliff, four hundred feet high, forms an angry promontory that juts into the Mediterranean. It's like a giant king's arrogant jaw. The monastery walls are off-white or cream colored. The roof is rusty brown. It's a large structure —it occupies the full breadth of the promontory. The south wall is flush to the cliff face.

I swallow, fight the urge to hurry to the monastery to get a better look. "Let's stick to our procedure," I say. "We don't want to miss anything."

Ellison smiles. "You heard the man," he tells Carlyle.

We crawl past the three-hundred-foot cliffs at thirty knots. Scan them for caves. At last, we reach Koitída Sofías. With the Sea Hawk at a hundred feet, the cliff and the monastery tower over us.

The lower cliffs east of the promontory form a crescent. At their base is a beautiful cove, a hundred yards wide at the mouth. The western end of the cove is flush to the high cliff that forms the promontory. There is no beach. The waters gently kiss the vertical walls.

Waves break against the base of the promontory and the cliffs far to the east. The cove, however, is peaceful. The waves rolling in from the south seem to interfere with each other and leave the cove undisturbed. The result is a beautifully tranquil bower.

"That's Bie Eirini," Ellison says. "It means Blue Peace. If there was any kind of beach down there, I'd hike over to see it."

"How can the water be so tranquil?"

"Geological accident. It probably wasn't tranquil for thousands of years. Over time, the corners of the cove were eroded. Now they provide the interference that makes the waters peaceful. In another thousand years, the tranquility will be gone."

I scan the walls of the promontory and the cliff face that cradles Bie Eirini. The crescent of tranquil water lies at the base of a jagged rock wall. It's as though the cliffs once formed a tall cylinder with the cove at the base. The cylinder was then cut in half from top to bottom. One side of the cylinder—the promontory—is a hundred feet taller than the rest.

"That's a big cove," I say. "No cave in there?"

Ellison shakes his head. "None that I can see. We come here often. Every time we pass, we stop for a few minutes."

I scan the rock face with my binoculars. "The height of the cliffs keeps Bie Eirini in shadow most of the day. You probably get the same view every time."

"We do." Ellison turns his attention to the monastery. "I wonder how much the owner paid for it."

"Can we orbit the monastery for a closer look?"

"The residents won't appreciate it," Ellison says. "I don't want Commander Palomas fielding complaints. They don't mind if we sightsee from a distance though. Greg, stand off a hundred yards and we'll glass the place."

The copilot takes us a hundred yards out to sea and climbs to four hundred feet. He hovers while Ellison and I study the monastery through our field glasses. It's a beautiful structure. Four stories high, measured from the top of the promontory. Long rows of windows. I make a mental note to research the structure of Greek monasteries when I get a chance. I wonder if the windows belong to individual rooms, or if the new owner has remodeled the interior.

There are more structures behind the one that overlooks

the ocean. Two smaller ones on the inland side. These are constructed so as to appear part of the main building. They were probably built at different times, hundreds of years apart, then grafted onto the original monastery.

I lean back in the gunner seat. "I could look at that place all day, but we need to finish this sweep."

"Alright," Ellison says. "Let's go."

We continue our painstaking search. By the time we reach the more built-up area around Ierapetra, we've covered every inch of cliff higher than sixty feet above sea level. The larger caves the aircrew showed me would have made great tourist attractions. Like the first two, they weren't big enough to hide a freighter.

The smaller caves, and there were many, were nonstarters.

"Shall we continue west?" Ellison asks.

The crew's tired, but they're game for more. I don't think it'll help to search farther west. Based on Stein's data, and Orlov's, Ierapetra was conservatively beyond the hijacked *Medusa*'s steaming radius.

All our search parameters have been conservative. Sixty feet is conservative. It would allow them to hide a dismasted *Medusa*.

I decided to search sixty-foot caves. Based on the assumption that the pirates want the gold, and are happy to chop the masts off the ship. *Medusa* is disposable.

The *Medusa*. A six-thousand-ton freighter.

Disposable.

"We don't go farther west," I say. "We do the sweep over again."

"Breed, we've been over every inch of those cliffs. Everything over sixty feet. There's nothing there."

"Ellison, in a world of ubiquitous ISR, where's the best place to hide a ship?"

The pilot twists in his seat. Blank, he stares at me.

"Satellites, drones, airplanes, helos. Nothing. But we know the *Medusa*'s steaming radius. We know she *has* to be here. Where's the best place to hide her?"

Ellison's eyes widen. "You mean..."

"They *scuttled* her."

Comprehension shoots through Ellison like adrenalin. "Reznick. Can we use that magnetometer to find a sunken ship?"

The ASW technician looks up. "It's straightforward. We can detect subs down to depths of three hundred and fifty feet. The strength of a magnetic field decays as the inverse cube of the distance. Deeper than that, the signal becomes far too attenuated."

Ellison cuts him off. "Three hundred and fifty feet is too deep for convenient salvage. Pull up charts of these waters."

"We're almost bingo fuel," Carlyle says.

"We got lots of daylight. Breed, we'll tank up at Souda Bay. While we're loading gas, we'll go over the charts. Define the parameters of a magnetic anomaly detector search."

Carlyle turns the Sea Hawk north-by-west, destination Souda Bay Navy Base. As we fly inland, the mountains of Crete rear up all around us. The copilot is running a gauntlet. To the east is a rough dragon's spine of peaks. Darker in hue than the ocean and sky, they appear as smears of blue and green across an impressionist's canvas.

To the west, a massive peak towers over us. The base of the mountain is so broad, the flanks of the cone slope gently to the summit. I'm struck by the arid countryside, the faded green of the lower slopes, and the ice cream white cap.

"This is the long way around." Ellison sounds half apologetic. "These peaks are over eight thousand feet. At those altitudes, our rotors lose efficiency. Flying at five thousand is below our ceiling, but we'll put less strain on the engines."

"All we have to do is avoid decorating the landscape," Carlyle says.

Helos in Afghanistan faced the same constraints. I relax and try to absorb the geography.

"What's the ice cream cone?" I ask.

"That's Mount Ida," Ellison says. "The tallest peak on the island. We'll swing north of the massif. Fly toward Heraklio, then turn west for the base. The peaks on the right are the Dikti and Tripti Mountains of the Lasithi region. They're two separate ranges, but from this angle, they overlap and look like one. Koitída Sofias is part of the southern Triptis."

Ellison turns his attention back to the instruments. The Sea Hawk flies on, and we fall into a comfortable silence.

I lean back in my seat. Fight down my excitement.

The answer was staring me in the face all along.

11

THE THIRD DAY – EARLY AFTERNOON, CRETE

Souda Bay Navy Base, on the north coast of Crete, is the largest NATO naval facility in the eastern Mediterranean. The imposing White Mountains of Crete present a magnificent backdrop. Operated by the Hellenic Navy, it's the only facility in the region capable of servicing a *Nimitz*-class super carrier.

There's one in port, with its Aegis defensive complement. One *Ticonderoga*-class cruiser and four Arleigh Burke destroyers.

The Sea Hawk squats like a huge dragonfly on the helideck of the USS *Pressley Bannon*. Lieutenant Carlyle supervises refueling while Ellison, Reznick and I go below. A Chief Petty Officer guides us to the Combat Information Center.

It's been a while since I was aboard this destroyer. At the time, she was under the command of Captain Abraham Cruik. A combat captain if ever there was one. Cut from the same cloth as John Paul Jones. *Give me a fast ship, for I intend to go in harm's way*. Cruik's been promoted to Rear Admiral.

He left the *Arleigh Burke*-class destroyer in the capable hands of his XO, Commander Katie Palomas. It's unusual to give an XO command of the ship on which they serve as first officer. Palomas will make Captain when she is given another command.

Nothing's changed on the *Pressley Bannon*. The crew is one hundred percent professional. Palomas was Cruik's protégé. High visibility arrows are painted on the decks in the passageways. Compartments are labeled on the deck, not their doors. If the ship is hit, the passageways will fill with smoke. Sailors can find their way crawling on their bellies. The *Pressley Bannon* is designed and run to take hits and keep fighting.

A Marine wearing a sidearm lets us into the CIC. Commander Palomas rises from her leather captain's chair and shakes my hand. "You're full of creative ideas, Breed."

Palomas is an attractive woman. Dark brown hair tied back in a severe bun, a fine figure in regulation Navy coveralls. Silver oak leaves glint on her lapels. Sailors sit at consoles in front of wall-to-wall screens that show the battlespace for hundreds of miles. At sea or in port, the *Pressley Bannon* is always on watch.

"This one should have hit me sooner, Commander. And I have not yet been proven right."

Palomas leads us to a wide plot table covered with charts. "It makes total sense," she says. "Keep in mind, they'll have to come back to salvage the gold."

"Yes, but they can do that at their leisure. I'm not sure how they plan to do it. Thirty tons of gold is a lot of heavy cargo. On the other hand, professional merchantmen deal with heavier cargoes all the time."

"True enough. How do you propose to conduct this search?"

I look from Ellison to Reznick. "We can narrow the search further. We have a haystack, now we look for the needle."

"With a magnetic anomaly detector," Ellison says.

"Yes. But we don't approach the problem linearly."

"What do you mean?"

"We set the parameters of the search. We know that the water has to be at least one hundred feet deep to cover the *Medusa* with masts intact. Let's say one hundred and twenty. But they would not have sunk her deeper than that. Because the pressure would be too great. It would complicate salvage efforts."

"Alright," Reznick says. "No deeper than one hundred and twenty feet. Twenty fathoms."

I remind myself that the helo crew are naval aviators. They think in terms of nautical units, while I think in terms of land units. A fathom is six feet.

"Let's have a look at the coast from Sitia to Ierapetra," I tell him. "I want you to draw a contour, off the coast, where the bottom is one hundred and twenty feet. Then, closer to shore, another contour, where the bottom is sixty feet."

"You're being conservative," Palomas says.

"Yes. The sixty-foot contour is the shallowest in case they have dismasted her. The one-hundred-and-twenty-foot contour is the deepest if her masts are intact."

Reznick taps furiously on his laptop keyboard. Calls up charts and discards them one after another. Finds one that satisfies him, zooms in on the Lasithi region. He taps some more, and the program traces two contour lines off the coast of Crete. One red, one blue. The red line is farther from shore. The blue line is closer. "That's your search corridor he says. Everything between the lines."

"There you have it," I say. "The distance varies with the slope of the bottom. The steeper the slope, the closer the lines are to shore. The more gentle the slope, the farther out they are."

"Why are the lines close together in some places and farther apart in others?" Palomas asks.

"That has to do with the steepness and concavity of the slope," Reznick says. "The steeper and more concave the slope, the closer the lines are to shore, and the closer the lines are to each other. The flatter and less concave the slope, the farther the lines are from shore, and the farther they are from each other."

"Do you think the distance from shore matters?" Ellison asks.

"I think it depends," I tell him, "on how they intend to salvage the gold. If they intend to shuttle it to shore in more than one trip, closer is better. If they intend to haul it up and put it on another ship, the distance to shore is irrelevant."

"They will want to avoid surface activity that looks like a salvage operation," Palomas says.

"Yes. It may be worthwhile to start our search in areas no more than two or three hundred yards from shore."

Reznick spreads a chart on the table. Covers it with an acetate overlay. Referring to his laptop, he draws the red and blue contours in colored grease pencil. "We should rule out the built-up areas," he says. "The big cities are out. So is everything within a mile on either side of coastal villages."

The ASW technician taps on his keyboard again. The program filters sections of the search corridor where the red line is more than three hundred yards from shore. We're left with five blocks. All are near the larger ports, and on the south coast of the Lasithi region.

Palomas frowns. "Of course the search area would be close to shore where there are deep-water ports."

"Yes, Commander. We will eliminate those." Reznick takes a black grease pencil. With violent slashes, he marks the acetate overlay. Blacks out the areas near busy ports and fishing villages. When he's done, we're left with five sections.

We stand around the table. Stare at the chart that may hold our last chance.

"We'll fly east to west," I say. "Skip over the blacked-out areas, focus on the search blocks. How do you use your magnetic anomaly detector?"

"It's mounted on the tail of the aircraft," Ellison says. "Reznick monitors it from his console and laptop. We have to fly low because the magnetic field can be very weak. One pass will ascertain whether anything is in the target area. If the target is of interest, we'll fly more passes to confirm its size and orientation."

"The new software is outstanding." Reznick's like a kid in shop class excited about his pet project. "Submarines are difficult because they're trying to evade us. If the target is stationary, our sensors can draw its picture in detail. The Navy degausses its ships. The Russians have started using non-magnetic titanium. A merchantman like *Medusa* is detectable. The problem is orientation."

"What do you mean?"

"The target's orientation affects the signal. If we fly perpendicular to the target's long axis, we'll get a brief signal. There and gone. We'll have to fly low and slow, investigate all contacts."

I turn to Ellison and Palomas. "In that case, we'd better

get started. Commander, I'll need a wetsuit, aqualung, and dive gear."

Palomas smiles. "That confident, are you?"

"Commander, if this doesn't work, I don't know *what* we'll do."

SEARCHING with the magnetic anomaly detector is slower and more painstaking than our visual search with binoculars. Ellison and Carlyle take turns at the controls. The concentration required to fly the narrow search corridor exhausts them.

The search is no less exhausting for Reznick. He sits like a sphinx, staring at his console. Occasionally, his eyes flick to the laptop to ensure we have not drifted from the channel. We cover the first block in the search corridor without a single contact.

"Are you sure it's working?" I ask.

"It's working," Reznick says. "I've tuned it to find large objects. A metal wrench won't set it off, but a sunken car will."

"We're coming up on the second block," Ellison calls.

Reznick turns back to his console.

Keller and I have little to do. We sit in silence, unwilling to indulge in small talk. I find my muscles knotting with tension. I'm tempted to call Stein and update her on our progress. Force myself not to. I don't want to get her hopes up. I'm excited by my theory. It will be a huge disappointment if we find nothing.

I turn my thoughts to Stein and Hecate. Hecate had been everything I expected in bed. Athletic, vigorous, all good fun.

We play-fought, wrestled, and fucked on the floor. We've got the carpet burns to show for it. Fought our way to the bed. Done everything a man and woman with healthy imaginations and no inhibitions could come up with. Finished with surprising tenderness and fallen asleep.

Stein troubles me. The attraction I feel is real, but fraught with neurotic complications. Stein's not like any woman I've ever met. Therein lies the attraction, and therein lies the world of hurt an encounter could lead to.

The sound of a buzzer drags me back to the helo.

"Contact," Reznick yells.

Ellison's at the controls. He cruises forward for a few seconds.

"Fading now," Reznick calls. "Come around one-eighty. Let's have another pass."

The pilot hovers, turns the Sea Hawk around, and retraces his path. Keller and I get up from our seats and stand on either side of Reznick and his console.

"There it is," Reznick says. The buzzer sounds again. It must be set to alert an operator who is nodding off. The ASW technician slaps a button and turns it off. "I make it seventy-five feet east to west."

The laptop screen shows a bright green capsule against a black background. That's it. A blur, seventy-five feet long.

"Can we do a run north to south, sir?"

"I'll give you two," Ellison says.

"One pass won't necessarily do it," Reznick explains. "We might fly off-center. Two passes and we should cover the target."

"Seventy-five feet is too small," I say.

"That's why we're running north to south now. We have to determine her dimensions."

Ellison makes the two passes. The green blob doesn't acquire any more detail. It remains a blurred green capsule.

"Dimensions seventy-five feet by fifteen," Reznick says. "I reckon coastal boat with a metal hull and wooden superstructure. That's why we aren't getting any detail. The wood isn't registering."

"It's not her." I bite back disappointment. Finding the *Medusa* right away was too much to ask.

"No," Reznick says. "The Med has very little tidal variation. She went down, got pushed here by a storm."

"Resuming search," Ellison calls. Then, to Carlyle, "Your aircraft."

Reznick turns back to his console. Keller and I return to our seats.

I stretch, do a leg isometric.

We find two more contacts in the next hour. Both too small to be *Medusa*, but we overfly them repeatedly and investigate in detail.

In the distance, Koitída Sofias stands in sharp relief against the ocean and cloudless sky. I'm grateful for the distraction. Tired of sitting in the helo with nothing useful to do. As we crawl closer, I take out my survival radio and snap some photographs. I try to frame them like tourist shots.

We fly past Bie Eirini. Carlyle is at the controls. Ellison is reclining in his seat, enjoying the view.

I'm jolted by the buzzer.

"Contact," Reznick calls. "There and gone."

"Hover," Ellison instructs Carlyle. "Reznick, was it real?"

"Yes, sir. Not my imagination, you heard the alarm."

"Very well. Greg, let's turn back. Go again."

The copilot turns the Sea Hawk. I grab one of the rails on Reznick's H-frame. Look down at his laptop. There's a fuzzy green dot on the screen. Another buzz. The green dot glows brighter, a hair thicker.

"Not much to write home about," I say.

Reznick ignores me. "There's something there, sir. Can we get a north to south pass?"

The copilot marks our location, flies toward the cliffs, and turns around. Slowly, he begins a north to south pass. Two hundred yards from the cliffs, the buzzer sounds again.

"Contact." Reznick can't keep the excitement from his voice. It's contagious—my muscles tense and I tighten my grip on the H-frame.

I watch the green blob lengthen. It grows into a long capsule. One end of the capsule faces Bie Eirini, the other faces the Med.

"We've got something," Reznick says. "It's a *big* fucker, sir."

Some things acquire reality without rational cognition. Sometimes, everything comes together and you *know*.

The way I *know* we've found the *Medusa*.

12

THE THIRD DAY – AFTERNOON, BIE EIRINI

Ellison takes over the controls. At thirty-five feet, he makes two more passes over Bie Eirini. South-to-north, perpendicular to the shore, then back again. "How's your signal?" he asks.

"Five-by-five." Reznick stares at his laptop screen. The program traces its three-dimensional plot on Cartesian XYZ axes. The first pass sketches a luminous green slug against a black background. "Length four hundred feet. Beam sixty. The vessel appears to be intact."

Those are the exact dimensions of the *Medusa*. I fight to control my excitement. "Can you improve the resolution?"

"That's what the second pass is for," Reznick says. "Remember, MAD will only reveal the metallic pieces of the hulk. Anything made of wood won't show up."

The program resets and starts to overlay detail on top of the slug's image. The slug starts to acquire definition. It looks like a ship, its bow pointed straight into Bie Eirini. The image is so detailed, we can see windlasses on the fo'c'sle and the links of anchor chains, fore and aft. The superstructure and cargo hatches are flat white slabs with green borders.

"We wouldn't get this much detail from a military vessel," Reznick says. "The Navy degausses the hulls. Merchant vessels don't bother."

"That's the *Medusa*." I turn toward Ellison. The pilot is hovering two hundred yards offshore. "Lieutenant Commander, I need to go down and confirm."

"Suit up," the pilot says. "When you're ready, I'll put you in."

I get into my wetsuit while Keller readies my aqualung. The water isn't that cold, but I worry about hurting myself on sharp rocks and other junk on the bottom. The neoprene wetsuit adds a layer of protection. "Give me two tanks," I tell him.

Weight belt on, I strap my Cold Steel OSS to my calf, hilt up. Keller hands me a waterproof flashlight that I clip to my belt. Then he helps me shrug on the aqualung and cinch the straps. I spit in my mask to keep it from fogging. Fasten the mask and fins over my chest. Bite down on the mouthpiece, take some breaths to test the airflow. If anything goes wrong, I'll be able to breathe.

"How deep is it?" I ask Reznick.

"Eighteen fathoms," the ASW technician says. "A bit over a hundred feet."

A hundred feet is a reasonable depth for an aqualung. I've gone a lot deeper in aqualungs, breathing mixed gasses. Combat Dive School trains you to use some fancy equipment. But... deeper than a hundred, hardhats are safer.

I give Keller a thumbs-up. The flight engineer turns to Ellison and speaks into his intercom. "Good to go."

The door is wide open. Things are getting real. The thunder of the rotors fades into background noise.

The pilot takes the Sea Hawk down until it is fifteen feet from the surface. Bie Eirini is living up to its name. The water is tranquil, there are no waves to speak of. Ellison looks back at me over his shoulder. He's done this hundreds of times. Now he's anticipating the weight displacement when two hundred pounds leaves his machine from one side. I flash him a thumbs-up.

I stand at the door and step from the helicopter. Step, not jump. If I jump, I'll add to Ellison's problem by introducing more unbalancing force as I leave. I look down at the blue ocean. This simple act maintains my kinesthesia—it keeps me oriented in freefall.

The water closes over me with a splash. I bob to the surface, where I'm engulfed in the Sea Hawk's prop wash. I bite my mouthpiece and suck air. Adjust my mask and put on my fins.

One last look at the helo, a quick wave to signal I'm okay. I nose over, swim toward the magnetic anomaly that can only be the *Medusa*.

I've jumped out of airplanes a thousand times, freefall is fun. I'm combat dive qualified, but I'm never as comfortable in the ocean. They say that to do extreme things requires the ability to switch off your imagination. I've never had to do that when I jump out of an airplane, climb a mountain, or drive a fast car. But the ocean is a different world altogether.

When I swim in the open ocean, I imagine seven miles of cold water beneath me. It's far worse than the thought of falling seven miles through empty space, waiting to open my parachute. The thought that I'm sharing the ocean with all kinds of unfamiliar ocean animals makes things worse.

In the ocean, I have to discipline my imagination.

Arms at my sides, I let my legs do the work.

The deeper you go, the more the water filters the different wavelengths of light. The phenomenon is on dramatic display when you dive with a buddy who wears a red wetsuit. Red is the first color to disappear. On the surface, the suit looks red. Go down a few feet, and it starts to look green. Deeper than a hundred feet, green shades into jade, then midnight blue. Below two hundred feet, nothing is left. The absence of color is black.

Where is it? The damn thing is supposed to be a hundred feet tall. All I can see are mottled shades of black and green. A rocky bottom.

Strong hands grab me. I thrash violently to free myself. A thick rope snags my mouthpiece. Threatens to tear away my life source. I grasp at the arms that restrain me. Find myself tangled in a net.

Terror strikes and my heart pounds. The greatest danger underwater is entanglement. That's why we're not supposed to dive alone.

I go completely still, force myself to relax. Sink a few feet, look around. I blundered into a fishing net. Not just any net. Large flaps of fabric have been attached to it in patches. With great care, I extricate myself. Rise a few feet, examine the obstacle.

It's camouflage. A modified fishing net. Certainly more than one. If I look through it, I can make out the hull of the freighter. The pirates must have scuttled her, then used fishing trawlers to lay nets over the hulk.

I pull myself hand-over-hand, follow the net to the bottom. There, I find loops in the net anchored with hooked steel spikes. The spikes must have been fired through the loops and into the bottom with high-powered compressed CO_2 guns. That's how they keep the current from shifting the net.

Big operation. More complex than I dreamed. I feel excitement that I was right, but a shadow of fear hangs over my shoulder. The pirates are well-financed and thoroughly professional. I should have known that from the advanced spoofing technology. This hijacking was a sophisticated heist. They scouted and prepared this location. Prepared the camouflage nets. Arranged for trawlers to lay it. Equipped divers with hardware to anchor it.

I draw my Cold Steel from its scabbard and hack at the net. Cut myself a hole six feet square to swim through. The work takes ten minutes. I swim through the hole, find myself cloaked in gloom. The camouflage patches obscure much of the light from the surface.

The *Medusa*'s single propeller towers above me. The ship settled on an even keel, and the big screw is twenty feet in diameter. I swim up past the name *MEDUSA*, painted in big white letters on the fantail. I rise to the level of the poop deck, grab a stanchion, and pull myself over.

It's just like the *Goliath*. I can make out the aft anchor chains, windlasses and paint lockers. Cargo hatches three and four stretch ahead of me on the well deck.

Let's see if the gold is still aboard. I swim to the super-structure and find the well deck door wide open. The interior is black. I unclip my flashlight and turn it on. Enter the compartment.

The starboard companionway leads to the overhead saloon. The port companionway leads to the holds. I'm conscious of the dangers involved in diving alone. If I run into trouble down there, I might never get out. Still, the ship was scuttled, not damaged in an accident. I doubt I'll run afoul of debris or wreckage.

I dive headfirst down the companionway, make my way to the aft holds. I focus my attention on what lies ahead, not the blackness that closes in behind me. In that blackness lie demons. Consistent with a deliberate scuttling, watertight doors everywhere have been propped open. Once they opened the seacocks, water poured in and evenly flooded the ship.

Number three and number four holds are occupied by endless rows of crates lashed with heavy straps and stacked on pallets. Harding-James described how the gold was packed. Plastic cases of four-hundred-ounce gold bars, forty bars to a pallet. Each pallet weighing half a ton and worth thirty-two million dollars. These pallets are too broad to carry gold. Crates this large, containing gold, would be too heavy to manage.

The gold isn't in number three or number four holds.

I turn around, swim back to the amidships compartments. Make my way past the open watertight doors, and the companionways leading up to the superstructure. I share the space with small fish. Some glide past my mask, heading in the opposite direction. Others pass me on my way forward.

There's another oval doorway that leads to number two hold. I swim through and play my light around the compartment. This one's full of heavy machinery. Earth-moving equipment, lashed to blocks bolted to the deck. Heavy-duty straps provide additional stability. The loadmasters were careful to ensure the weight would not shift in heavy seas. It does not do to upset the trim of a vessel.

Ahead is number one hold. I've looked everywhere else, that's where the gold will be stored. I kick forward, sweep my

light from side to side. I haven't travelled half the length of
the compartment before my way is obstructed by a hulking
piece of machinery.

I stop and play my light on the object. It's a massive excavator, fifteen or twenty tons. Its cleated metal tracks block
two-thirds the width of the compartment. They're secured
with heavy-duty steel clamps. The excavator has a raised
glassed-in cab for the operator. The articulated digging arm,
with its clawed bucket, looks obscenely human. It's bent at
the elbow to fold against the chassis for storage. The whole
affair is secured with a web of long canvas straps.

There, caught in the crook of the mechanical arm, is an
object that shines white in my light. It's moving in the gentle
current. I duck under a strap and kick toward the shiny
mass. It looks like a white volleyball, smooth and glossy.
There's a gray, leathery mass attached to one side.

I reach forward, try to lift it for a better view.

The object is fleshy, slippery. I recoil. It's a human skull.
It must be a man, by its size. Most of the hair and scalp have
sloughed off. The corpse is in an advanced state of decomposition. The cells have broken down, loosening the surface
layers of skin. My attempt to grip the volleyball caused the
last tissue of melted flesh to come away in my fingers.
Bleached eyebrows and eyelids slide off hollow eye sockets.
A foul-looking black fluid flows from the lipless mouth and
hangs suspended in the water.

I choke down a scream. The leathery thing clinging to
the side of the object unfurls like the petals of a grotesque
flower. It's an octopus. Its malevolent eyes shine in my light.
Each arm, equipped with its own brain, waves. None of them
like to have their meal interrupted.

Thrash backward. Bump into the strap. Play the light on

the thing trapped in the crook of the excavator's arm. It's a corpse. So bloated by the gasses of decomposition that it burst its clothing like a balloon. Floated from where it lay on the deck and got caught in the machinery. The bloating doubled its size, wedged it in the excavator.

Of course. The *Medusa* has been missing long enough for the murdered crew to decompose and come to the surface. It happens all the time when airplanes go down over water, or when ships sink. Bodies float free of the wreckage. They're spotted by aircraft, drones, satellites or passing ships. Hellenic Navy search and rescue found nothing. American and Russian satellites found nothing. American drones found nothing.

These men haven't floated to the surface.

Because they were murdered in number two hold.

Heart pounding, I swim under the strap and retreat to the amidships bulkhead. Play my flashlight across the overhead. How many corpses? At least two dozen. They are all there—the murdered crew and security detail. All floated free of the deck. Unrecognizable, festooned with octopi feasting on their bleached flesh.

I fight down panic. I've seen worse. The charnel-houses of battlefields. Corpses that could not be evacuated under fire decomposed where they fell. I've hauled dead men from shallow graves only to have the flesh of their wrists come away in my hands. Soft tissue liquefying with decay.

This horror took me by surprise. I force myself to breathe regularly. Relax my muscles. Study the corpses to learn what I can. There isn't much to tell. Several bodies wear load-bearing vests crammed with magazines. The security detail. Disarmed, then executed with the crew. The vests, secured with Velcro buckles, didn't tear from the pressure. The expanding corpses extruded from the arm and neck holes. I look down. Spent brass litters the deck.

Enough of this. I'm tempted to search number one hold, but I've seen more than enough. The gold has to be there. No way am I swimming back through this sunken graveyard if I can avoid it.

I retreat to the superstructure and swim up the companionway to the well deck. The layout is so much like the *Goliath* that the *Medusa* could be her sister ship. They were built in the same shipyard, years apart. I use the internal companionway to make my way through the superstructure. The saloon is empty. A television set, a bare sofa. The cushions have floated away. I steel myself against another ghastly discovery, play my light across the overhead. Thank God, no bodies, just sofa cushions.

One level higher, I enter the bridge deck. I didn't take this route when I explored the *Goliath*. Work my way forward, check left and right. The captain's day cabin is empty, as is the radio operator's. I swim forward, find the navigation compartment empty.

To my right is the radio compartment. Two corpses. Advanced decomposition, food for fishes. The bridge is high on the hulk. Open to the sea via the port and starboard wings. Crabs and other bottom feeders scuttle on the deck. They cover unrecognizable fleshy... *things*. Based on his location, one corpse must have been the radio operator. The other is unrecognizable but his uniform jacket marks him as an officer. The captain, perhaps, working with the radio operator to transmit a Mayday before they were cut down.

I back out of the radio compartment and swim onto the bridge. There's something odd. Lights flicker on the other side of the bridge windows. Instinctively, I douse my flashlight. Stare through the glass.

Beneath the camouflage net, a team of half a dozen scuba divers work around number one hold. Next to the open hatch, they've erected an electric crane. Bolted it to the deck. The lifting device has hoisted a pallet from deep within the bowels of the *Medusa*.

Right away, I recognize the pallets Harding-James described. Gold bars in transparent plastic boxes, pallets two feet square. Forty bars per pallet, each pallet half a ton. The *Medusa* is carrying thirty tons, so there must be sixty pallets.

The divers maneuver a sea sleigh into position next to the pallet. This is a modern sea sleigh, fifteen feet long, with two electric propellers. Room for two pilots in the cockpit. The crane hoists the pallet and positions it over the center of the sleigh. The divers work on either side, directing the crane operator. A yellow square and cross have been painted on the center of the cargo bed. The divers guide the pallet so that it covers the square.

Sea sleighs were originally designed to propel two-ton torpedoes into enemy battleships. Back in the day, they were ridden into battle by more-or-less expendable divers. Nowadays, sleighs are often remotely operated drones, used for the same purpose.

The point is, these modern sea sleighs are able to carry half-ton pallets of gold bullion. Flying a sea sleigh underwater is a lot like flying an airplane. The trim of the platform is important. The distribution of weight along the length of the sleigh affects the pilot's ability to control the vehicle. That's why the pallet was carefully placed on a predetermined point on the cargo bed. The vehicle's trim has been precisely calculated.

The divers swim to the net and swing open a patch of camouflage. The opening allows the sea sleigh to pass. The platform, laden with thirty-two million dollars worth of gold, sets off for the coast. I would bet my life they're stacking the gold on a hidden dock.

Slowly, the sea sleigh disappears into the gloom. The remaining divers swim back into number one hold. I was lucky. The corpses in number two discouraged me from swimming into number one. I would have blundered into the divers at work. Right now, they are preparing the next pallet for salvage.

Sixty pallets, two billion dollars. How many have they already moved? The sea sleigh has to cover two hundred yards to the coast and then return. Hoisting the pallets from the hold is painstaking work. Damaging the crane would jeopardize the operation.

There has to be a cave on the coast. Worn into the belly of Bie Eirini thousands of years ago. That four-hundred-foot half-cylinder of rock keeps the cove in perpetual shadow. Only light coming from the south will illuminate the interior. That never happens because the sun travels east to west. When directly overhead, the tranquil waters are lit bright blue, but not the shadowy cliffs.

The pirates have proven themselves masters of camouflage. Canvas tarps painted with black and brown streaks hung over the cave mouth. If the cave is big enough, they might have installed wooden doors that can be opened and shut to allow small ships to enter. Divers and sea sleighs. The outer doors can also be painted with camouflage patterns.

I decide to leave the way I came, through the superstructure and over the stern well deck. I push away from the windows and turn in the water.

A long, slender object flashes past my face mask. It clangs into the bulkhead next to me, bounces off, and sinks to the deck. It's a barbed harpoon. Missed me by an inch.

My attacker is standing in the doorway to the starboard wing. A pirate in a black wetsuit. Carrying a high-powered, compressed CO_2 speargun. I draw my Cold Steel from its sheath and launch myself at him.

The pirate doesn't have time to reload from the quiver strapped to his aqualung. He draws a shark knife and kicks toward me. I deflect his wide, roundhouse slash with my left forearm. Go for his belly with my own blade. We both struggle to adapt to underwater combat. The water resistance slows our movements. Enough to make it necessary to adjust our thought processes.

He catches my wrist in his left hand. I twist toward his thumb, break free.

We're bumping face masks. One of us is going to die in the next thirty seconds. He tries to stab me, this time close-in. He's holding the shark knife blade down and I close my left fist around it.

Shocked, he grabs my shoulder with his left hand, tries to jerk his knife free of my grip. I thrust the Cold Steel behind his chin, up through his mouth and palate. First I feel the point go into soft flesh. Then, with a crunch, I punch through bone. Feel the pointed, double-edged blade sink into spongy brain tissue. His eyes widen and his mouth opens in a soundless scream. The flat of my blade glints behind his teeth. Bubbles erupt from his mouthpiece.

I don't dare let go of his knife. He's dying, but I won't take the chance he'll stab me in his death throes. I twist the Cold Steel in his jaw, further into his brain, jerk it around to destroy as much tissue as possible. I feel the blade scraping bone. It's like pithing a frog. He's dead, but neurons continue to fire, flushing chemicals across synapses. His arms and legs convulse.

Throw myself on the pirate, pin his body to the deck. Fucker's still twitching. I grope for the dead man's tank, shut off his air flow. Pray the pirates on the forward well deck didn't notice the burst of bubbles. This man must have noticed my light flicking behind the bridge windows. Came to investigate without alerting his friends.

I jerk the Cold Steel from his brain. A small cloud of midnight blue blood issues from his mouth and the hole under his chin. I sheath my knife and look out the bridge windows. The pirates continue their work on the well deck.

Grab his aqualung harness, drag him off the bridge, and float him into the radio compartment.

Clench my left fist. Adrenaline's wearing off, and salt water in an open cut isn't pleasant. I swim the length of the bridge deck. Follow the companionway down to the saloon. The portholes are open, but too small to get through. I shine my light ahead of me and descend another level.

I switch off the flashlight and swim back across the well deck. This time I keep my head on a swivel. I could cut a new hole in the net, but I don't want to get caught while I'm at it. Instead, I dive over the fantail, do a flip, and allow myself to sink to the bottom. Swim away from the propeller to the hole I cut earlier.

Check my watch. I've been down over half an hour. What did Reznick say? Eighteen fathoms. I think back to combat dive school. The rule of 120 says your time on the bottom plus your depth can't exceed 120 without requiring a decompression stop. At a hundred feet and half an hour, I'm past that. I can't go shooting to the surface.

I force myself to ascend slowly. Monitor the pressure in my ears. At fifty feet, I stop. Check my watch, wait for three minutes. Ascend to fifteen feet, wait three minutes more. Maybe it's not necessary, but safe is better than dead.

Break the surface, raise my mask. The Sea Hawk is hovering a short distance away. I wave, and Ellison dips toward me. Keller is at the door, operating the hydraulic hoist. He lowers a bright orange jacket to me, and I push my arms through it. Flash a thumbs-up, wait to be pulled aboard.

"What happened to your hand?" Keller asks.

I sit on the floor of the Sea Hawk, pull off my fins. "Bad company," I tell him. "Let me talk to the pilot."

Keller hands me headphones with an intercom set. Opens a first-aid kit and bandages my hand. I address Ellison. "It's the *Medusa*," I tell him. "No question. The hijackers are shifting the cargo. Patch me through to Stein."

The copilot fiddles with the radios while I strip off the wetsuit and get dressed.

"I can't raise her," the copilot says.

Damn. "Okay, take me back to Ésperos. Get me Commander Palomas."

I stuff my Mark 23 into my waistband, strap the Cold Steel to my calf, jerk my pants leg down over it. The survival radio goes in my right hip pocket, spare mags in the left. Slip on my deck shoes.

"Breed." Katie Palomas sounds tense. "What have you found?"

"The *Medusa*," I tell her. "Scuttled in eighteen fathoms. Intact, settled on an even keel. The pirates laid camouflage nets over her. They are transferring the gold right now. Shuttling it to a camouflaged cave in Bie Eirini. I reckon there's a dock inside."

"Then we have them. We're weighing anchor now. We'll arrive shortly after midnight."

"Alright. Commander, I need to circle back to Stein. I'll pick her up and rendezvous with the *Pressley Bannon*. Best request a SEAL team."

Ellison tips the Sea Hawk slightly nose-down and heads for Rhodes. Keller sits in the jump seat between the pilots, and I belt myself into the gunner seat next to the open door. The tranquility of Bie Eirini belies the violence that occurred beneath the surface.

I take out my survival radio. Push buttons through the laminated case, scroll to Stein's entry on the contact list. The screen flashes: *Connecting*.

After thirty seconds, the message changes: *Failed to connect*. I shake my head, squeeze the radio back into my pocket.

I shift my gaze to Koitída Sofías, the monastery high on the cliff. It's a breathtaking sight. The sun is on its way down and the windows blaze with orange fire.

The monastery dwindles in the distance. I rest the back of my head against the headrest and hold up my bandaged hand. Flex my fingers, test their mobility. I feel pain, but the range of movement has not been impaired. My body remains one hundred percent functional.

I raise my other arm. Streaks of rust from the man I killed have crusted on the back of my hand. The seawater has not rinsed it away. Again, I flex my fingers. Feel the strength of the musculature. I remember shoving the Cold Steel into the man's brain. These are my hands. They know how to kill. I don't even need to tell them what to do.

I think of octopi, with brains in each of their arms. The arms hunt and kill independently, yet with the same objective of nourishing the beast.

We're approaching the endgame.

Ellison's voice cuts into my reverie. "The Huey is still on the pad."

I turn in my seat and look forward, past Keller, at Ésperos. Ellison's right, the Huey is still sitting on the helipad. But the hairs rise on the back of my neck. The scene has changed. The *Grigoro Fidi* is gone.

"Where's the yacht?" I ask.

"I don't know. It's a fast boat. In the time we've been away, it could have gone anywhere."

"Put me down," I tell him, "then stand off two miles. I'll call you."

"Roger that."

Ellison guides the Sea Hawk toward the beach. The spot where he picked me up. We're at a thousand feet, descending to four hundred. My eyes search the estate. I see Kyrios's security force at the main gate. A couple of men on the terrace of the big house.

Why isn't Stein responding?

We overfly the bluffs that overlook the beach. At five hundred feet, there's a bright flash from the top.

Keller and I see the flash at the same time. "Incoming," he calls. "Four o'clock low."

The Sea Hawk turns hard. From flare buckets mounted on the fuselage, Ellison launches countermeasures. The flares burn hot to divert heat-seeking missiles. They arc like fireworks to either side of the Sea Hawk. Helos don't turn like jets. They're more vulnerable because they're sluggish. In the rear compartment, we're thrown against our straps.

I'm looking out the door as Ellison rights the helo. The missile flies past the countermeasures, its smoke trail white against the darkening sky. For a second, I allow myself to breathe.

"Another one!" Keller yells. "Seven o'clock!"

Ellison pitches the Sea Hawk in the opposite direction. Launches more countermeasures. This time, the machine does not respond quickly enough. A terrible crash knocks the helo to one side and I'm thrown hard against the straps.

"*Pressley Bannon*," the copilot calls, "this is Blue King Five. We've taken a Stinger off Ésperos."

A voice crackles in my ears. It's the *Pressley Bannon*. "Say status, Blue King Five."

Ellison has straightened the Sea Hawk. "Keller, Reznick. Watch for more anti-air."

The flight engineer and ASW technician release their belts and lurch to the door, look down at the bluffs. Keller grips the articulated minigun on the starboard side. "Nothing yet," he says. "I count three guys on the bluff with rifles."

"If you get a clear shot, waste 'em."

"Roger that." Keller swings the minigun to the door.

"We got hit in the boom." Ellison tests his stick and pedals. "I think we're flyable. I'm going to try to put her down."

"We're flyable," the copilot says into the radio. "We're going to put her down. There are bad guys with rifles on the cliff."

Ellison cranes his neck, looking for a landing spot. The terrain around Ésperos is rugged. Apart from the helipad, occupied by the Huey, the only flat ground in sight is the two-hundred-yard stretch of beach. The pilot aims to put it down as far from the gunmen as possible.

G3 battle rifles are effective to twelve hundred yards. I grip the edge of my seat. Given a choice between dying in a twisted airframe and dodging bullets, I'd rather dodge bullets.

Keller traverses the minigun, prepares to fire.

There's an earsplitting crack behind us. It's not an explosion. Something mechanical in the tail assembly broke. Some kind of catastrophic failure. Instantly, the Sea Hawk enters a clockwise spin.

"Mayday, Mayday." The copilot doesn't wait for Ellison. The pilot is wrestling with the controls. He's got the left pedal jammed to the floor. The pedals control the pitch of the rear rotor, which counters the torque from the main set of blades. The clockwise spin suggests we've lost the stabilizer. The fact that Ellison's foot is on the floor with no effect confirms it. "This is Blue King Five. We've lost the tail rotor. We're going in."

It's impossible to describe the forces generated by an eighteen-thousand-pound helicopter that's spinning at fifty revolutions per minute. You're strapped to a giant animal that's whipping you around, and you're powerless to do anything about it.

Ellison is struggling to reach the power levers. "Shut them down, Greg! Shut them down!"

The torque from the main rotor is spinning us. The centrifugal force throws me forward against my straps. My eyes meet those of Keller, then flick to Reznick. They're pinned on either side of the open door. The world whirls before my eyes. Images of blue ocean and black rock alternately flash past. In seconds, we're spinning so fast the detail disappears. All I see through the door is a two-toned shutter —half black, half blue.

Ellison and the copilot struggle to switch off the Sea Hawk's engines. If they kill the rotors, they'll relieve the torque on the airframe.

"I can't reach them!" The copilot is fighting G-forces many times his body weight.

"We've got to!" Ellison struggles to lift his gloved hand. It might as well be a mile from the power levers.

I shut my eyes. Carlyle's voice rings in my ears. "Mayday, Mayday. Blue King Five. Going in, Ésperos beach."

The world has become a blur. I'm pinned against the straps. There's a terrific impact. For a brief instant, the insides of my eyelids flare bright red.

Then the lights go out.

13

Water surges through the open door. Sloshes around my legs. I don't claw my way back to consciousness. I wake up as though the light has been switched on.

The seats have all collapsed. My seat slid down the H-frame rails. On these helos, the seats crush down on impact. This creates a shock-absorbing effect to protect the occupants. The Apache and the Black Hawk are built the same way. These seats probably saved our lives.

Intentional or not, the Sea Hawk came down in the surf. We're a hundred yards from the beach, sinking fast.

"I couldn't reach them." Carlyle's still stunned, looking up at the power levers. Water is pouring through his door. It's already chest high.

"Bail out," Ellison says.

Keller shakes his head as though to clear it. The water level has risen to our necks. The flight engineer splashes out the door, paddles away from the helo. Carlyle opens his own door and exits the aircraft as it slips below the waves.

I gulp air as we sink, hold my breath. Open my eyes underwater. Reznick plants his hands on the edge of the door and drags himself out of the sinking helo. My eyes sting. My scuba gear is rolling around on the deck in the back of the compartment. I release the straps holding me to the H-frame. Grab the mask, put it on, blow it clear.

Clearing the mask cost me breath. I look toward the cockpit. Carlyle has egressed through his door. Ellison is struggling with his own door, can't get it open. The impact bent the frame. He gives up and levers himself out of his seat. Swings his left leg over the cyclic, reaches for the copilot's door.

We're going to make it. I swim through the open door and kick for the surface. Gulp air, look around.

Flat on his back, Carlyle bobs in the water. He's only a couple of feet away, and I splash to him. Grab his arm, pull him toward me. He turns his head, and his eyes meet mine. There are thwacking sounds and bullets smack into his chest and throat. High-powered rounds from a G3, full metal jacket. His eyes turn skyward and lose focus.

I jerk and splash away from him. Bullets slap the water where I had been. I hear the crack of G3s firing. Look around. A bullet blows off the top of Keller's head. A black object—skull and scalp—flies into the air. Reznick panics, swims for shore. Bullets stitch his back and he founders in the surf.

Gulp air, dive. Bullets leave cavitation trails as they decelerate in the water. This close to the surface, they're still going fast enough to kill me. I kick hard—force myself to go deeper.

I see the Sea Hawk on the bottom. A hundred yards out, the water can't be more than thirty feet deep. Ellison is egressing through the copilot's door, kicking for the surface.

I grab Ellison. His eyes are open and he stares at me through my mask. I shake my head violently, draw my finger across my throat. He doesn't understand, tries to surface a second time. Again, I restrain him.

The pilots have emergency oxygen bottles strapped to their legs. The HEED—Helicopter Emergency Egress Device—supplies a pilot with three minutes of emergency air in the event of a crash. I reach for the HEED holster on Ellison's leg and pull the D-ring. Pull the regulator head and hand it to him.

Ellison pushes the purge button to clear the regulator, sucks air. I grab him by the front of his flight suit and draw him deeper. We swim into the cabin of the sunken helicopter. Still holding my breath, I locate my aqualung and pull the harness straps over my shirt. Clear the regulator and suck air.

I don my weight belt, cinch it tight over the Mark 23. Lead Ellison from the interior of the Sea Hawk and swim underwater *toward* the pirates' bluff. They'll expect us to swim away. I imagine them scanning the surface for any sign of me coming up for air. They don't know Ellison got out of the helo, and they might have hit me. At a range of two hundred yards, they won't see our bubble trails.

Ellison has only three minutes oxygen, and it will take us ten or fifteen minutes to reach the rocky beach at the foot of the bluff. Sure enough, he runs out of air. I take my mouthpiece and give it to him. He fills his lungs and hands it back to me. Buddy-breathing, we continue underwater, swimming for the bluff. It's tempting to cut directly to shore. Twice,

Ellison pulls me in that direction, but I shake my head sternly. Point in the direction of the bluff.

We'll be sitting ducks on the beach. I want to come up among the rocks, right under the bluff. If possible, *behind* the bluff.

I slow our pace, force us to move deliberately. Ellison's panic subsides and he gets used to the buddy-breathing routine. We follow the bottom, making our way through forests of sea grass. The blades wave languidly in the current.

It's twenty minutes before I feel safe enough to lead Ellison to the shore. The bottom becomes rockier. We have to be careful not to cut or scrape ourselves on the rocks. The bottom slopes gently upward. I poke my head up to check our position.

We're behind the bluffs. Exactly where I want to be. I raise my face to the sky. Pirates on the bluff will be lit by the setting sun. They're nowhere to be seen. Probably on the other side of the bluff, looking down on the crash site. How long will they wait? After twenty minutes, they're probably getting impatient. But they can't discount the possibility that I've found an air bubble trapped in the Sea Hawk's hulk.

I lead Ellison to the shelter of craggy boulders at the foot of the bluff. We crouch low, and I shrug off the aqualung and mask. We're soaked through. I lift my shirt, pull the Mark 23 from my waistband.

The pistol is waterlogged. I drop the magazine and set it upside-down on a rock. Rack the slide open, catch the extracted bullet before it hits the ground. Do a three-point check, turn the weapon muzzle-down and drain the barrel. Satisfied, I snick the loose round back in the magazine and slide it into the butt of the pistol. Release the slide, decock, good to go.

"Wait here."

I leave Ellison among the rocks. Stare up at the bluff, pick my line. The top is two hundred feet away. Exhausting, but not technically difficult. More like climbing a steep hill than climbing a mountain. The slope is well-lit by the setting sun. I move deliberately, careful not to dislodge loose rock. There's no sign of the gunmen, and I don't want to make any noise.

Their voices carry to me long before I reach the top. I can't understand a word, but they're arguing. It's not a full-on fight, but they're debating amongst themselves. It's not hard to guess what about. They know they killed three men, but they don't know where I've gone, or how many were in the helo. Helos usually have a crew of three or four. I could be dead, my body on the bottom. I could be hiding in the hulk, alive in an air bubble. I could be waiting them out. They're annoyed. How long do they have to wait?

When I get to the top, I lie prone. Peer around some rocks, evaluate the opposition.

Three men, all carrying G3 battle rifles. They're at the edge of the bluff, looking out to sea. The man in the middle stands upright, rifle cradled in his arms. Big guy wearing jeans, a long-sleeved black T-shirt, and a black Navy watch cap.

To his left, another man sits with his back to the ocean, rifle across his knees. This man is skinny and sharp-featured. He wears a beard and mustache, pointy at the ends. He looks lazy. Probably arguing that they should leave. In front of him lies the olive drab carrying cases of the Stingers they used on us.

The third man is on the right, lying prone. His rifle is to his shoulder, trained on the ocean.

I rise and stride toward the group.

The sitting man looks up, and his eyes widen. With the sun behind me, I appear to him as a straight black silhouette. The Mark 23 is held in my right hand, low, by my leg. I must look like the angel of death.

I raise the Mark 23 and shoot the standing man twice in the back, right between the shoulder blades. He pitches forward and falls facedown across his rifle.

The seated man starts to raise his weapon. This guy has the G3 resting across his knees. He has to lift it and aim. I shoot him between the eyes before he can react. A black hole appears above his nose. The back of his skull explodes into a glittering red and white halo.

The third man rolls on his side, looks back at me. He's in a hopeless position, his rifle pointed the wrong way. Think about it. The G3 is a long rifle, comparable to the FAL. It takes a long time to swing a thirty-six-inch weapon around and point it at anything that isn't right in front of you. Pistols are better offensive weapons at close quarters.

I step forward and shoot him twice. Once in the left temple, again in the left ear. I turn to the man I shot in the back. Put a third round into the back of his head.

Offshore, there's a small debris field where the Sea Hawk went down. The waves have carried a body to the beach. Facedown, arms splayed out, rolling gently with the waves. I can't tell who it is.

Three-for-three, but it's a bad trade. Any one of our guys was worth a hundred of these. I pull the survival radio from my pocket. Select the *Pressley Bannon*.

A male voice crackles from the speaker. "This is a US Navy channel. Identify yourself."

"This is Breed. Put Commander Palomas on."

Palomas cuts in, "Breed. What's your status?"

"We were ambushed, Commander. Three pirates on the bluff with G3s and a Stinger. Ellison crash-landed in the sea. We all got out, but the pirates shot three crew. Ellison and I are alive. I killed the pirates."

"Our other Sea Hawk is on the way," Palomas says.

"The three KIA are in the water," I tell her. "One has washed up on the beach. Kyrios's yacht, the *Grigoro Fidi*, is gone and we can't raise Stein."

"The *Pressley Bannon* is steaming to Bie Eirini."

"Ellison and I are going to check out Ésperos. Kyrios's security force is still in place."

"Breed, how do you know they're friendly?"

"I don't. But I have to find out what happened to Stein and Harding-James."

"Do you think Kyrios is in on it?"

"I don't know. It is possible. If you encounter the *Fidi*, you have to treat her with suspicion."

I feel sick to my stomach. Excited about finding the *Medusa*, I neglected the possibility that the monastery might be occupied by the pirates. They would have watched the Sea Hawk fly search passes over Bie Eirini. Watched me dive on the hulk, watched me return and fly off in the helicopter. They warned pirates on Rhodes, instructed them to set the ambush.

"Understood. Keep me informed."

Palomas signs off. I'm sick with worry about Stein. She trusted Kyrios and Hecate. That might have been her undoing.

I reach down and pick up the sitting man's G3. Sling it over my shoulder, relieve him of a canvas bandolier of spare magazines. Turn and pick my way over the reverse slope. Ellison is waiting.

14

THE THIRD DAY – EARLY EVENING, ÉSPEROS

Ellison and I approach Ésperos over the bluffs. The arid, rocky landscape is sprinkled with old olive trees. We pick our way two hundred yards to the estate.

The white wall that protects Ésperos extends only to the edge of the cliff. The paths to the beach are covered by armed security guards. The men I saw standing on the terrace guard the approach. They must have seen the pirates shoot us down. The only question is—were they in on the ambush?

A small barred gate is set in the wall. There are four armed men at the main gate, using a Land Rover as a road-block. Kyrios's men won't leave the side entrances unguarded. There are closed-circuit TV cameras mounted on the walls. Those are monitored by men inside the estate. Where are the men on the front line?

There's only one way to find out. I lead Ellison to a dusty olive tree. The tree squats in a field littered with everything from stones to small boulders. I make the pilot lie at the base of the tree, Hand him the G3, spare magazines, and my survival radio.

"I'm going to talk to the security force," I tell him. "I don't know if they were in on the ambush. You stay here."

"I'll cover you."

"No. Don't fire unless they come after you. If they take me, let them. Call Commander Palomas, wait for her to send help. If everything is okay, I'll wave you over."

I leave Ellison at the tree. Run in a low crouch toward the edge of the cliff. I don't want to make it easy for anyone at the estate to locate the pilot. When I've achieved a measure of separation, I straighten and walk toward the gate.

The cameras over the side gate turn toward me. Follow my progress.

Reckon I'll go knock on the door.

Before I reach the gate, it opens, and two men step out. They wear load-bearing vests and carry M4 carbines. Squad tactical radios are Velcroed to their left shoulders. They're hardened, ex-military. One man, bearded, looks older than the other.

"You're Breed," the bearded man says. His English is accented. He speaks it with confidence.

"Yes. How do you know?"

"I watched you arrive with Ms Hecate yesterday. Her security detail told us what happened on the road."

"Did you see what happened a while ago?"

"We saw them shoot down your helicopter, yes. I saw it pick you up this morning." The man looks toward the tree where Ellison is hiding. "Tell your friend to come out. You have nothing to fear from us."

"You didn't know the pirates were there?"

"Of course not. There is going to be trouble from this."

I turn and wave to Ellison. The pilot stands up and walks toward us. "Those men killed three American aviators," I tell him. "Another helicopter is coming to collect the bodies."

"We didn't know how many were killed. We realized there were survivors when we heard gunshots from the top."

Ellison joins us.

"Where are my friends?" I ask the bearded man. "Where are Mr Kyrios and Hecate?"

"They all departed in the *Grigoro Fidi* some time ago."

"I don't understand. Why?"

The man shrugs. "Mr Kyrios does not explain his comings and goings."

Something's wrong. The *Fidi* must have left while I was diving on the *Medusa*. There are no coincidences. Someone in that monastery reported that we had found the bullion ship. I don't want to believe Hecate's involved, but her father? It's his yacht.

"Who exactly departed on the *Fidi*?"

"Mr Kyrios, Ms Hecate, Mr Drakos. Also, Ms Stein and the Englishman."

Drakos. The scion of a dynasty of smugglers and gun-runners. A dynasty that stretches back generations. But the Kyrios dynasty distanced itself from the Drakos dynasty long ago.

"Bodyguards?"

"Mr Drakos brought his security."

"What about Mr Kyrios and Hecate?"

"We remain at Ésperos. When Mr Kyrios travels on the *Grigoro Fidi*, he relies on the crew. They are quite capable."

"How many men with Mr Drakos?"

"Six."

I turn to Ellison. "Can you fly a Huey?"

"Yes. It's a vintage muscle car. The Sea Hawk is a digital wonder."

"Can you land it on the *Pressley Bannon*?"

"Yes. The Huey's not equipped for the bear trap, but these seas are calm enough."

The bear trap is a device used to help helicopters land in rough seas.

I turn to the bearded man. "Mr Kyrios and my friends are in danger," I tell him. "We need to borrow your helicopter. If necessary, the United States Navy will compensate you."

The man laughs. "Compensate Mr Kyrios? He could *buy* the United States Navy! Take what you want."

ELLISON and I race west in the Huey. The sky is aflame with the setting sun. I adjust my headset and contact the *Pressley Bannon*. I'm handed to Palomas.

"Breed, what have you found?"

"The *Grigoro Fidi* left Ésperos with Kyrios, his daughter, and a hard character named Drakos. He's a wealthy Greek businessman. His family has a reputation for smuggling and gun-running. I think he's behind the hijacking. Probably forced Kyrios to go along with it."

"What about Stein and Harding-James?"

"They're aboard the *Fidi*. We have to assume they are hostages. That ship is full of armed men. Kyrios and Drakos both have bodyguards. The *Grigoro Fidi* itself is loaded with small arms and rockets. Javelins, Stingers, the works."

Ellison taps me on the shoulder. Points ahead.

The *Pressley Bannon*'s other Sea Hawk is roaring toward

us. It's a black speck silhouetted against the blazing sky. It grows in size with every passing second.

"We have your second Sea Hawk in sight," I tell Palomas. "Kyrios's bodyguards are expecting them at Ésperos."

The Sea Hawk and the Huey pass each other at over three hundred knots closure. I glimpse men in the doors, hands on the miniguns. I worry more for the safety of the bodyguards than the airmen. With Blue King Five down, and three of their shipmates dead, the gunners are not going to be in the mood to take chances.

"What is that yacht doing loaded with weapons?" Palomas can't keep the outrage from her voice.

"Kyrios is something of a character. His grandfather was driven out of Turkiye in 1920. The Turkish army shot his grandmother. He's been terrified of being rendered stateless ever since. He has money stashed all over the world and a hundred escape routes. The *Grigoro Fidi* is one of them. It has four gas turbine engines and does fifty knots."

"He got a head start on us," Palomas says. "Probably been at Bie Eirini for hours. I'll say this, Breed. If he comes out, we will interdict."

"I don't think he's the mastermind, Commander. Drakos has something on him. Kyrios and his daughter may be hostages, just like Stein and Harding-James."

"We'll stop them first, figure it out after. What do *you* want, Breed?"

"I think Drakos's men have transferred the gold from the *Medusa* to an ocean cave in Bie Eirini. They're going to put the gold on the *Fidi* and make a run for it."

"We've taken aboard a platoon of SEALs. Come dawn, they will storm Bie Eirini. If Drakos runs, we will interdict."

"What are the Greeks going to say?"

"I have authorization from Sixth Fleet, and they have authorization from SECNAV. SECNAV has liaised with State and the Hellenic authorities."

If it's good enough for Palomas, it's good enough for me.

"The SEALs can't go in guns blazing. They have to reconnoiter the cove first. We're only *guessing* there's a cave."

"Doubting yourself, Breed?"

"No. Following procedures. The SEAL commander will too."

"He told me the same thing. We'll send a pathfinder team before the *Pressley Bannon* gets within visual range. The scouts will report before we launch the main force."

"Give me till dawn, Commander."

"What will you do with that time, Breed?"

"I'm going for Stein and Harding-James. Might even get some intel to make the SEALs' job easier."

"Alright, Breed. You have till dawn."

I swallow hard. Tell the Commander what I'll need.

Palomas tells me I'm crazy.

15

THE THIRD DAY – EVENING, USS PRESSLEY BANNON

I sit with Commander Katie Palomas in a cramped compartment off her CIC. The air is cool and smells faintly of metal and electronic equipment. A sailor has a laptop open. Its screen is mirrored to a large high-definition display. He's showing the pictures of Koitída Sofias and Bie Eirini that I took earlier in the day.

"I don't see a cave," Palomas says.

"The pirates have camouflaged it. I *saw* divers carrying gold in sea sleighs. Straight into Bie Eirini."

"Why can't you penetrate the monastery from inland?"

The photograph we are looking at was shot with Blue King Five hovering two hundred yards off Koitída Sofias.

"It's a promontory. If you look from above, you'll see it's like the tip of your finger jutting out to sea. The promontory is a hundred feet above the surrounding cliffs. An elevated position. Monasteries were built like forts. Monks were guardians of valuable manuscripts, jewelry, and religious art. They had to protect themselves from attack by brigands, mercenaries and bankrupt rulers. The northern approach will be heavily defended. That makes the south face the best bet."

"Can you climb it? That face is four hundred feet high. The monastery wall is flush with the edge and another sixty feet above that."

I put my hand on the sailor's shoulder and bend close to the screen.

"Can you let me draw on that screen?"

"Use this stylus, sir."

He slides me a tablet and stylus. I pick it up and trace an orange line on the image. Follow a vertical seam in the rock that begins at the base and rises to the monastery.

"That crack looks like it will take me straight up the cliff." I lift the stylus from the tablet. "Zoom in."

The sailor taps and magnifies the image. We're able to view the seam more clearly.

"It looks promising." With the tip of the stylus, I point to a dark line that extends horizontally from the seam to a vertical gash in the rock. "Look at that shelf there."

"That's a shelf? How wide is it?"

"Hard to say. If it's more than a few inches, it could be enough. That vertical gash to the right is a natural chimney."

"It's wide."

"Yes. I reckon a man can fit inside it."

"The walls look sheer."

"Assault climbers do tougher ascents."

"In the dark?"

"Yes. And I'll bring a set of NODs—Night Optical Devices—with me."

"How do you plan to get there? You won't get close with a helo. We know they have Stingers."

A helicopter insertion at the monastery is out of the

question. Kyrios's armory on the *Grigoro Fidi* is proof. The war in Ukraine has scattered Stingers and Javelins all over the black market. The pirates have effective air defense. That leaves land attack from the north, or a mountain assault from the south. After the day's events, the pirates will be on the alert. The south cliff is more vulnerable.

I don't have all the details, but I have a good sense of the situation.

Kyrios's yacht *had* to have headed for Bie Eirini. If I'm right, the plan was to shift the gold from the *Medusa* to a hidden cave under the cliff. The pirates would then have transferred the bullion to another vessel, probably under cover of darkness. That transfer would have taken place at their leisure.

Drakos probably planned the heist. He intended to take the gold away in trawlers, or some larger ship. I'd forced his hand by locating the *Medusa*. His men in the monastery reported a US Navy helo dropped Breed into Bie Eirini. He had to move.

The *Grigoro Fidi* was the fastest ship available. Kyrios and his crew were at hand. I don't know how he did it, but Drakos and his men seized the vessel. Probably held Kyrios and Hecate at gunpoint. Stein and the crew would have been helpless. The call from the monastery came while I was underwater. Drakos and his hostages were underway before I was back in the Sea Hawk.

A helo can't land me *on* the monastery, but it can get me close enough.

"Lieutenant Commander Ellison can land me downwind of Koitída Sofias. At least a mile, and out of sight. I'll hike to the base of the cliff."

"I couldn't find everything you asked for."

"What could you get?"

"Rope and pitons."

"None of the other climbing gear?"

"Breed, this is a warship. You can have all the rope you want, any kind you want. I got you three-eighths-inch, dynamic unicore. Six hundred feet in three lengths of two hundred. That other stuff? We found the *one* sailor who went climbing in the Dolomites last year. He's crazy about climbing. Insists the only real climbing is climbing that's done with equipment from the nineteen-twenties. Rambled on about Mallory and Irvine and people I never heard of. Didn't have *any* of that stuff you asked for. He's got pitons and a hammer."

"No nuts and cams?"

"Afraid not. I'll show you the gear."

"Do the SEALs have anything?"

"They laughed."

I push annoyance aside. That a US Navy warship like the USS *Pressley Bannon* would carry modern climbing equipment in its stores had been unlikely from the start. It was unfortunate that Palomas had weighed anchor before I learned the *Grigoro Fidi* was gone. There might have been more gear available at Souda Bay.

"Let me see the gear, Commander."

Palomas leads me to the helicopter hangar. It's empty. Both Sea Hawks are gone, and the Huey is lashed to the helideck. A ruck and collection of equipment sits on the deck next to one of the bulkheads. A young officer lays a half-shell helmet and a set of NODs next to the pack.

"Ensign Clavano," Palomas says. "This is Mr Breed. I see the SEALs did come up with something."

The officer looks too young to shave. He salutes Palomas

and shakes my hand. "Yes, ma'am. The NODs are in good working order. Checked them myself. They gave me a few other items. They're in with the rest."

I pick up the ruck. The climbing enthusiast has provided a chalk bag. That's good. A webbed climbing harness. A hammer and fifteen pounds of karabiners and iron pitons.

Climbing shoes were too much of an ask, and my deck shoes are worthless. Palomas found me two pairs of cross-fit trainers. I try both pairs, pick the most comfortable. The SEALs also provided a holster for a Mark 23 and two spare magazines.

Palomas weighs a piton in her hand. "Wouldn't it be easier to fire a grapnel over the top with a rope attached?"

"That works in the movies. Can you imagine breaking a window, or having the iron land in someone's drink?"

It's not everything I asked for, but it's enough. Modern climbing protection like nuts and cams were developed to preserve rock. The popularity of sport climbing means most faces would crumble from assaults with thousands of pitons. Pitons haven't dominated an assault climber's gear for decades. I prefer pitons to modern protection. The iron makes me feel like I'm conquering the rock.

I enjoyed the Special Forces Assault Climbers Course. Special Forces are trained to lead mountain operations. We are the first troops on the face—we mark the route. Often, we climb faces that have never been climbed before. We determine the most effective lines of attack, secure marshaling areas. We set protection and prepare ropes for the waves of mountain troops that follow.

My friends and I continued climbing after graduation from the Assault Climbers Course. We gravitated to traditional climbing rather than sport climbing. Special Forces attracts men who are into the extreme. A lot of Green Berets went into skydiving after the Military Freefall Course. I did civilian skydiving early, to prepare myself for airborne training. After the Assault Climbers Course, we tried free soloing—climbing without the protection of a rope. I tried a few easy pitches, but that was all. For me, the reward-to-risk ratio wasn't there.

It's likely no one's climbed the cliff to Koitída Sofias. That makes it a terrific face for an assault climber.

I pick up a length of rope, flex it for suppleness. The coil probably weighs eight pounds. Three coils, let's say twenty-five pounds to be conservative.

"I need three lightweight bags," I tell Palomas. "One for each coil. The bags should have an adjustable shoulder strap. Ideally, a zippered flap at one end, but a zippered closure in any case."

Palomas looks at the ensign. "Ensign Clavano, you heard the man."

"Yes, ma'am." The boy runs from the hangar.

Katie Palomas shakes her head. "I remember when I graduated the Academy. Was I ever *that* young?"

"We all have misplaced childhoods."

I return Palomas's scowl with a smile.

The door to the hangar opens and a man in Navy khakis enters. He wears the two silver bars of an O-3, a Navy lieutenant. Pinned to his chest is a gold SEAL trident.

Palomas returns the SEAL lieutenant's salute. "Breed, this is Lieutenant Morgan. He commands the SEAL platoon that will be raiding Bie Eirini."

"What can you tell me about the opposition, Breed?"

"Ruthless, well armed. Out of the water, they carry H&K

G3s, MP5s, and USPs. Underwater, I have seen high-powered, compressed CO_2 spearguns."

"Strength?"

"Unknown. I've killed six. There could easily be two or three dozen more."

"What can you tell us about this underwater cave?"

"I am guessing that it is there, but it is an educated guess. I have seen the pirates shuttling half-ton pallets of gold bullion from the *Medusa* to Bie Eirini."

"Any idea how big it is?"

"No. I've seen other caves on this coast a hundred feet high and just as wide. It would not be difficult to camouflage the mouth of such a cave. The pirates have proven themselves skilled at camouflage."

"Why are *you* going after the monastery?"

"I think there are high value targets and hostages in Koitída Sofías. They won't store the gold there, it's too heavy to carry up. No, they're waiting to transfer it to a ship."

"I understand there's a high-speed yacht in the area."

"I think it's already there."

Morgan plants his hands on his hips. "I'm going to scout the beach," he says. "We'll find the cave, attack at dawn."

"Just remember you have friendlies in there."

"Come meet my platoon. I want them all to know you on sight."

16

THE THIRD DAY – LATE EVENING, KOITÍDA SOFIAS

Underway, the USS *Pressley Bannon* knifes through the waters of the Aegean. Ellison takes off and retraces the first leg of the route we flew earlier. We overfly Heraklio, then leave it behind, a sparkling forest of lights.

The sky is clear, an ocean of stars. Ahead of us lies Mount Ida. The peak's cap glows a luminous blue-white in the moonlight. The landscape below is black, save for the odd light from a goatherd's hut. To the east, the Dikti range and its dominant peak of Mount Spathi appear midnight blue against the lighter night sky. To the west lie Souda Bay and the White Mountains. The range is as striking as Mount Ida, a long series of dark peaks capped by fields of snow that glisten in the icy moonlight.

Ellison has been assigned a replacement copilot from the destroyer. The Kyrios helicopter was purchased in commercial configuration. The compartment behind the cockpit has been arranged with six comfortable bucket seats. I sit in the center, behind and between the pilots.

My helmet and NODs rest on the seat next to me. Three zippered nylon rope bags lie on the deck at my feet. I lean forward and stare at the horizon. The pilots' faces are bathed in the dim glow of the Huey's instruments.

"You really going to climb that cliff in the dark?" Ellison asks.

"It won't be pitch black," I tell him. "You'll be surprised how much light you can get from the moon, especially if you allow your night vision to adjust. And I'm carrying NODs."

"The wind is moderate, east-to-west," Ellison says. "We'll fly to the coast, then dog-leg east. I'll put down on the beach, a mile from Koitída Sofías. They won't see or hear us."

I keep my expression blank, but the prospect of climbing to Koitída Sofías tickles my stomach. It's a good case of nerves—the kind that focuses a man's attention.

In daylight, the cliff would be little more than an interesting exercise. At night it might prove insurmountable. In theory, the two routes I've identified are climbable. In practice, I won't know until I arrive and test the rock. The vertical crack in the middle is the most direct route, a single pitch. The chimney to the east looks tempting, but will require a potentially difficult traverse.

"Sure you got enough rope?" Ellison asks.

I appreciate Ellison's banter. "Yes, sir. Three bags full."

Climbing alone is very different from climbing with a partner. It's naturally more risky, but one also has to carry everything up the rock himself.

Special Forces assault climbers usually work in pairs. The more skilled climber acts as "lead" and is the first to ascend the pitch. His partner, referred to as the "second," remains at the bottom of the face. The second manages the supply of rope. He forms a belay—he holds the rope securely, so he can support the lead if the lead should fall. As the lead ascends, the second pays out rope. The lead then hammers pitons into the rock and clips the rope to the support points.

When the lead comes to his first desired objective, he builds an anchor—a strong support point. He then uses the rope to pull up the team's equipment. Belays his second from above, while the man climbs to join him. Finally, the team haul up the rope and begin the process again.

The point is—when you lead an assault team, you leave most of the rope with your second.

"Climbing alone is tough," I say. "You have to carry all your rope with you. I reckon the cliff and monastery are five hundred feet high. I've got six hundred feet in three bags, two hundred feet to a bag. Enough for the climb *and* a traverse if I need it."

The copilot turns his head. Looks at the rope bags on the floor, the iron I'm carrying racked to my waist. "That gear must weigh a ton."

I'm not carrying a rifle. The H&K Mark 23 was designed as an offensive pistol for special operations missions in close quarters. I wear it at my right hip, holstered on a pistol belt, with four spare magazines.

Where I used to wear a load-bearing vest and plate carrier, I've buckled on the climbing harness. The sailor who climbed the Dolomites must be small and wiry—I had to adjust the straps. Around my waist, the rack of iron. Pitons, two piton hammers, karabiners, and quick-draws. Quick-draws consist of two karabiners joined by a short cord. The chalk bag is behind my holster, close to where my right hand falls.

"The iron weighs twenty pounds. Forty-five with the

rope. With weapons, canteen, helmet and NODs, I'm carrying fifty in total. The good news is—I plan to leave rope and iron behind as I climb."

"How's that work?"

"I carry the rope bags on my back. Instead of a second man belaying me from below, I tie one end of the first rope to an anchor. Maybe a tree, maybe spikes I pound into rock at the bottom. I climb and pay out the rope from the bag. Feed the rope through an arresting device."

"Arresting device?"

"It's meant to grab the rope if you fall. As I climb, I install protection. Let's say... twenty feet up, I hammer in a piton and clip my rope to it with a quick-draw. The rope runs freely through the quick-draw's karabiner so I can keep climbing.

"Now suppose I climb ten feet above the piton and fall off the face. I fall the ten feet to the piton and then fall ten more. The arresting device attached to my harness grabs the rope and keeps more from paying out from the bag. If the piton holds, my weight will be supported by the rope that runs from my harness to the piton, and then to the anchor on the ground."

"So you fall twenty feet."

"That's right. It's still a hard fall to take. Let's say you climb a long way up, setting pitons every ten feet. If you fall, and the last piton you set doesn't hold, you fall past the next one and hope *that* holds. Then you'll have fallen forty feet. Either of those falls is enough to cause a severe injury."

Climbing alone is dangerous, but not unusual. Special Forces assault climbers work in teams, but train to complete their missions alone if one is injured.

Two is one, one is none.

Until one man's killed or wounded. There could be a battalion of mountain troops waiting at the foot of the mountain. Waiting for a route to be identified, marshaling areas marked, climbing ropes prepared. Missions must be completed on schedule, alone if necessary.

We trained to operate alone.

The flutter in my stomach changes from apprehension to anticipation.

It can be done.

ELLISON PUTS me down on a deserted stretch of beach two thousand yards from Koitída Sofías. He promises to make one or two passes well north and east of the monastery. If the pirates hear the Huey fly upwind, their attention will be drawn to the north approach.

We hope.

The beach is thirty yards wide. The smooth sand stretches from the creamy surf of the Mediterranean to a low bluff.

One thing I can do well is ruck. Delta Force, Combat Applications Group, First Special Forces Detachment Delta. Whatever you want to call it today, the unit's operators have the wiry strength and endurance of pack mules. I've completed forced marches with heavier loads. Climbing with this one will be a challenge, but not outside my envelope.

I cover the beach at a fast pace, stretching my stride. The rack of pitons on my hip rattles and slaps against my thigh. The NODs I flip up on the half-shell helmet. My eyes have adapted to the moonlit tableau, and the binocular NODs are notorious for restricting peripheral vision.

Before long, the ground becomes more difficult. The visibility is alright, but I find myself hiking on a narrow storm beach strewn with rocks. Waves from the Mediterranean have driven them onto the shore. The bluff to the north rises to a moderately steep cliff. The closer I get to Koitída Sofias and Bie Eirini, the narrower the beach will become, and the taller the cliffs.

I hike as close as I can to the wall to reduce my exposure. It's a tradeoff. From the cliff, larger boulders have tumbled onto the beach. The closer I get to the wall, the more difficult the obstacle course. I keep my eyes on the rock and sand to make sure I don't fall and twist an ankle. As I expected, the moonlight casts the beach and rocky cliffs into icy relief.

My thoughts turn to the odd cast of characters waiting for me at Koitída Sofias. Stein is the most familiar. We've known each other professionally for years. The attraction between us is beginning to intrude on that relationship. The scene this morning at Ésperos was a bit much. The behavior she displayed at the party last night was just far enough over the top to make me wonder. Stein, the woman, is far more emotional than Stein the Deputy Director.

Should I allow myself to give in to the attraction, or keep everything professional?

Stein gets a vote.

Then, there's Hecate. We've slept together once, and already we're heavily "in like." She's all woman, and I feel caught in her gravitational field. And she in mine. Last night was fun, but we're from different worlds, and I doubt this will go anywhere.

The mission, the mission.

There are three others up there. Harding-James came along to recover his investment. I bet he wishes he'd stayed in London. Kyrios is something else. He's a hardened businessman, with a charming *Zorba the Greek* shtick.

Those were Stingers I saw in the *Grigoro Fidi*'s armory. Our Sea Hawk was shot down by a Stinger. I tell myself there are no coincidences. And yet... Kyrios is right. The Afghan and Ukraine wars have scattered those missiles everywhere. I could buy one in any high school parking lot.

Could Kyrios be involved? If he is, what does that say about Hecate?

Drakos is something else. I have no trouble imagining the big Greek as a pirate. Kyrios's father took the family fleet legitimate. I've heard nothing to suggest that Drakos and his family have left the smuggling business. And he took six bodyguards onto the *Grigoro Fidi*.

Lieutenant Morgan and his SEALs know what they'll be facing when they hit Bie Eirini in the morning. Their mission is to recover the gold. I have to find out what's going on with Drakos and Kyrios.

The cliffs to the north are now fully three hundred feet high and dangerously steep. A man can run up the first thirty feet at the base, but the grade steepens quickly. The limestone is black in the night. I'm feeling cautiously confident. The weather, always a concern when climbing, is fine. The sky is free of clouds, the moon is bright, the rock is dry. The land above the cliffs is dry. Plane trees are scattered far back from the edge. The rock is free of slippery vegetation.

I find myself walking straight toward a solid rock wall. The storm beach has curved to my right. I slow to a cautious walk and follow the curve. In spots the beach is so narrow that the gentle waves cream against the rocks and splash my shoes.

The wall rises vertically from the beach. I put my hand out to steady myself. Find the rock dry and hard. The consistency is good. Sometimes rock feels brittle or friable. That kind of rock will not hold iron.

Stone has always felt good under my hands. A worthy test of the strength in my fingers, wrists and arms. When I hold a rock, a rifle, or a woman in my hands, I'm reminded of my tactile nature.

Again, excitement flutters in my stomach.

I step around the curl of the wall. Come face-to-face with Koitída Sofías.

THE MONASTERY IS ONLY a hundred yards away. It lies ahead of me and to my right because the promontory juts into the Mediterranean. Bie Eirini is on the other side. Instinctively, I search the ocean for any sign of the *Grigoro Fidi* or the *Pressley Bannon.*

Neither vessel is visible. The destroyer will wait over the horizon until dawn. The SEALs can't swim that far underwater. The latest *Arleigh Burke*-class carries an SDV—a SEAL delivery vehicle. It's a mini-submarine that can maneuver the SEALs into swimming range undetected.

Grigoro Fidi is a mystery. For the first time, I wonder if I've guessed wrong. Perhaps Drakos and Kyrios did not take the yacht to Koitída Sofías. If not, where did they go?

I stare at the monastery. The structure stretches along the top of the four-hundred-foot cliff. The wall is sheer. I

need to work my way around to the south face. There lie my
climbing routes.

Cautiously, I close the distance to the base of the promontory. My clothing is dark, so I will not stand out. There are no
sentries visible. The monastery is less a castle than a normal
building. There are no turrets, ramparts or crenellations.
Rather, it has regular roofs and long rows of windows. The
windows are dark. Some rows of balconies have been recessed
into the wall, supported by the structure below. Other rows of
balconies protrude from the wall in cantilevers, supported by
brackets. The different styles of balcony are evidence that the
wings of the structure were built decades or centuries apart.

Slow and deliberate, I make my way across the base of
the promontory. With every step, I check the narrow storm
beach ahead of me and the walls of the cliff above. Already, I
can see the walls are so sheer it will be difficult for a casual
observer in the monastery to spot me. He would have to lean
out from a balcony and peer directly down the face.

I adjust the weight of the rope bags on my shoulders. I'm
at the foot of the south face. The moonlight is falling from
high on my left. It shines on the wall, causing irregularities
to cast deep shadows. I need to find the crack that stretches
to the monastery. It will be my highway for at least the first
two hundred feet. To find it, I need a good view of the face.

Stepping back would be ideal, but would require wading
into the Med. I flip down my binocular NODs, turn them on,
and adjust the focus. Looking through NODs is like staring
through a pair of drinking straws. You have no peripheral
vision. I focus on the wall, turn my head left and right.

The south face lights up green. I focus my attention
thirty feet up the pitch and slowly turn my head, left to right.

I look through the NODs and examine every feature. The wall extends a good hundred yards, west to east, and I'm standing at the western end.

I didn't think this would be such a slow process. I walk along the base of the wall, looking down to check my footing. Every few steps, I look up and continue my scan. Force myself to be patient.

The NODs peel back the shadows. Reveal cracks and seams in the wall. The crack I'm looking for will look like a vertical tectonic fissure. In the moonlight, one side of the wall will be raised and will cast a sharp shadow across the other. Under the NODs, the shadow will open up, revealing a seam that I can follow.

I cover the wall at a British slow march. Force myself to focus on the face. Koitída Sofías glowers at me like a muscular beast. On the scree, my legs ache from fighting to keep my balance. My neck stiffens from craning it skyward.

There! In the circular green glow of the NODs, a black vertical slash extends from seven o'clock to one o'clock. I blink, flip up the binoculars, and examine the wall by moonlight. The slash is not quite a vertical line, but it definitely extends the height of the face. I flip the NODs down, examine the crack more closely. Search higher for the horizontal ledge two hundred feet up. The ledge that leads to the natural chimney.

I can't see the ledge. Is this the right seam? Yes, it is. The ledge isn't visible because the moonlight falls on it from the side. It casts no shadow. There is nothing to create the kind of contrast that catches one's eye.

Time to go to work.

I flip up the NODs, step to the face, and search for a likely place to set an anchor. There are no trees on the beach, just boulders and rubble shaken loose from the wall. Greece is an earthquake-prone land. Crete has been created by a confluence of tectonic plates. It was the crashing together of those plates that created the White Mountains. I worry about the risk of falling rocks.

I decide to build my anchor on the base of the wall itself. I use two pitons, so if one fails, there is a backup. One piton I hammer into the seam, the other into a crack. I unzip my first rope bag. Secure the end of the rope to the first piton with a figure eight. Run it through the second and tie a clove hitch.

From a pocket, I draw a Prusik. It's a length of rope tied into a friction knot. The Prusik has been in use since Austrian climbers popularized it in 1931. I use it to tie the rope into my harness. When unloaded, the Prusik allows the rope to slide back and forth. If I come off the face, and my body weight loads the knot, the knot will friction-lock and arrest my fall.

I turn, unzip my fly, and piss into the Mediterranean. Take time to drain the dragon.

The left tube on my NODs, I set to close focus. The right tube, I focus on my feet. I tighten my chin strap and make sure my helmet sits comfortably. Then, I reach for chalk and powder my hands. Check that my gear is where it should be. I flip down my NODs, pick my first objective, and estimate the amount of rope I'll need to reach it. Flip the nods onto the crown of my helmet.

Good to go.

I step to the face and start to climb.

I CLIMB the first thirty feet without NODs. The moonlight is fine, and it's easy to find handholds and footholds around the seam. I hammer in a piton, secure a quick-draw, and clip in.

Koitída Sofías follows my progress with malevolent eyes.

After climbing a hundred feet, I grasp a vertical handhold in the crack, lean back, and rest my right arm. On either side of me, the wall is an ebonite slate. The moonlight shines on the ocean, as far as the eye can see. From this height, I can see farther along the horizon than at sea level. I wonder if I can see the *Pressley Bannon*. I see the lights of a couple of ships to the south and west.

Commander Palomas won't let her vessel be seen. She knows the monastery is four hundred feet up. She'll have done a quick calculation to determine how far the destroyer should stand off. I can't see her, but it is comforting to know she is there. Already, the SEAL delivery vehicle is on the way with Lieutenant Morgan's pathfinders.

Somewhere to my right, I hear a rattle. A rock has fallen from above and bounced down the face. The fall line is probably twenty or thirty feet to my right. I look up at the monastery, scan the face. No idea where the rock came from. I strain my ears, but hear nothing more.

I turn back to the wall and continue to climb.

A hundred feet up, the game changes. The crack I'm following is like two plates pushed against each other. The edges don't match, and the mismatch creates the seam. The face to the left begins to slope outward. The face to the right slopes in. The distance from the left edge to the right face widens. The moonlight casts a longer shadow. The crack, always an impenetrable black, becomes indistinguishable from a large swathe of the right face.

I can't see well enough to place pitons. Can't find hand or footholds.

With my left hand, I grope for the crack. The face on the right is smooth, and there's no lip against which to curl my fingers. I exhale, feel my way around inside the crack. Toward the top, it narrows a bit. I slide my hand deeper, clench my fist, pull.

The sides of the crack lock against my left fist. It's a hand-hold—sort of. My fist takes my weight. I let go with my right hand, flip down my NODs. The blackness of the face is replaced by a view through two drinking straws. When I look at the rock face, the view through the right tube is shocking in its clarity. The view through the left is a blur. When I look at my hands, the left tube snaps into focus and the right tube blurs.

I breathe slowly, allow my brain to adjust to the visual mismatch.

Climbing with NODs is not a straightforward exercise. In fact, the Army's field manual on assault climbing specifically states that while the pathfinder team should be equipped with NODs, they are not to use the devices on the climb. The FM does not state *why* pathfinders are discouraged from using NODs. I reckon it is partly due to the reduction in peripheral vision—to zero. That, and the problems with focus that must be dealt with.

Special Forces professionals feel compelled to master the use of available tools. In defiance of the field manual, I proceeded to use NODs as much as possible to push the envelope.

The problem with NODs is that at times you have to focus on your hands. For that, you need the close focus setting. At other times, you have to focus on your feet. At such times, you disengage close focus. This makes manipulation of the NODs clumsy, which slows your progress.

I find that by focusing one tube on my hands and the other on my feet, I can easily switch tubes depending on where I want to look. This solution is effective. However, it introduces two more issues. First, it further reduces your peripheral vision. Second, when you rely on one eye, you lose depth perception. Both issues are manageable. Like everything in life, the more you practice, the better you get.

I push higher, using my NODs to find the narrowest finger and toeholds. Slow is fast. I move deliberately, rehearse every movement in my mind before executing. Blink sweat out of my eyes. Realize I'm drenched.

Climbing uses every muscle in your body. It's a cliché to say you find muscles you never knew you had, but clichés become clichés because they're true. The handholds and footholds stress every sinew in your fingers, arms and legs. You cling to the face until your body quakes in agony.

My back arches. The only way to powder my hands in this spot is to wedge my entire body into the crack. Bend like a bow, look through my right NODs tube. My brain ignores the blurred view through my left tube while I find a foothold. I cross my legs, apply pressure against the foothold with my left trainer, squeeze my back against the side of the left face. The brace is formed by outward pressure to the left against my back and outward pressure to the right against my foot. Hands free, I reach for the chalk.

I push away the thought of what will happen if my training shoe slips. Focus on the task at hand.

At two hundred feet, I find the ledge. In the moonlight, its flat surface appears lighter than the face around it.

Eighteen inches wide, the ledge stretches fifty feet. I'm

not interested in the ledge for itself. I care about the natural chimney it connects to. Anything to push this climb along. I'm halfway there. If that chimney is half as good as it looks in the photograph, the home stretch will be easy.

The chimney is where I expect to find it. Connected to the ledge, it runs vertically on the face, parallel to the seam I've been following. I can't tell much about the chimney because I'm so close to the face. The chimney is a gamble, but it's worth it. The question is—can I get to it?

Evidence of the natural forces that created the ledge are there for me to see. The face next to the ledge is perfectly vertical. There is a horizontal seam between the eighteen-inch ledge and the face. The seam is so straight, it might have been cut by an engineer.

Thousands of years ago, a flat sheet of limestone above the ledge was shaken loose from the cliff. It might have been an earthquake in a land of earthquakes. It might have been the weight of the face putting stress on the rock underneath. For whatever reason, that sheet came off the face and tumbled to the storm beach below. The break was so clean, it left the ledge behind.

The ledge leads to the chimney. There is danger on that ledge. I have no idea what the limestone above the fallen sheet of rock is like. There is every chance it is friable rock that could come loose under its own weight.

Earlier, I heard a rock come off and rattle down the face. Its fall line is consistent with the section of cliff above the shelf. Weather, falling rock—those are what we call *objective hazards*. Some mountains are full of such risks. If I have to face a cliff with only one, I can live with it. I study the face by moonlight, then through the right tube of my NODs. I can study the problem all night, or I can go to work.

I go to work.

NOW EMPTY, the first rope bag flutters down the face. I pound a second piton into the crack above the last. Open my second bag, withdraw a length of rope. Build a second anchor on the two pitons, test its strength. It's firm against upward, downward, and lateral force. If I'm to traverse this ledge, it *has* to hold against lateral force.

I once talked with a roughneck who built skyscrapers in New York. Asked him how he could walk on those beams and girders thirty stories in the air. He told me it was no problem. Lay the girder on the street and you can walk along it without a second thought.

Most people who say they are afraid of heights are *not* afraid of heights. They are afraid of dying. Those are two different things. The man who flies in a passenger plane and looks out the window at the landscape thirty-six thousand feet below is not scared of heights. Put that same man at the edge of a skyscraper and have him look down, and he'll tell you he's afraid of heights. What he's *really* afraid of is falling to his death, which is perfectly rational. Everybody's afraid to die. But he's *not* afraid of heights.

The point is—if you feel safe, you won't feel afraid. The way to feel safe is to ensure you have thought everything through and have adequate protection.

I fasten myself onto the rope with a Prusik and spread myself flat against the wall. I feel the surface of the stone face and inch onto the ledge. I begin to move sideways, watch my step through the right tube of my NODs. It's easy going. I'm confident I can complete the fifty-foot traverse in five minutes if I don't stop.

Force myself to stop, fifteen feet onto the ledge. Slow is fast. I find a crack in the wall and hammer in a piton. It should take both lateral and downward force. Clip myself into it with a quick-draw, keep going.

There's a strange whistle in the air. Half whistle, half flutter. A blow on my left shoulder. It's like I've been clubbed from above. I'm so shocked that I grunt. More from surprise than pain. My torso twists counter-clockwise. Not a lot, but enough to throw the weight of my packs and the rack of irons to one side.

I'm falling off the face.

Jumping out of airplanes is something I've done so many times I've lost count. A thousand jumps or more. This is the same feeling. I'm coming off the ledge, going into freefall. The difference is, I know my descent is going to be arrested by the Prusik sling, the piton I just set, and the anchor fifteen feet behind me at the vertical crack.

This is why the anchor needs to take lateral force. Because I'm moving sideways along the ledge, the anchor is positioned at the same horizontal level as my last piton. When my safety rope engages that piton, my weight will apply downward force to the piton, which will be translated into lateral force against the anchor.

I crash against the wall with a tooth-rattling impact.

Ping!

A sharp, metallic sound. The piton didn't hold.

Now I'm afraid.

17

THE FOURTH DAY – MIDNIGHT, KOITÍDA
SOFIAS

I'm not dead yet.

After clipping into the last piton, I advanced ten feet farther along the ledge. The total length of rope separating me from the anchor is twenty-five feet. The anchor has become the pivot of a pendulum with a twenty-five-foot arm, and me dangling on the end.

Gravity drags me along the pendulum's arc. I bounce and scrape along the rock face, grunting with every impact. I reach the equilibrium point directly below the anchor and bump over the left-hand edge of the crack. Scrape farther along the left face, reach the pendulum's maximum angular displacement.

For a second, everything comes to a stop. My fingers grasp for purchase on the wall. Find none. Gravity resumes its remorseless work. I plunge again. Swearing under my breath, I arc in the opposite direction. Tuck in, try to minimize injury until physics brings me to a stop.

Twice more, I swing through arcs of decreasing angular

displacement. Finally, I come to rest against the wall, twenty-five feet below the anchor. I grip the crack with my left hand and the rope with my right. Close my eyes and sweat.

Check the Breed Machine. Not long ago, my muscles were in agony. Now my bones and teeth hurt. I don't think anything is broken. My shoulder must have been hit by a falling rock. I should have been more alert.

I cling to the rope with my right hand. Raise my left arm, extend and move it about. The arm feels alright, but the top of my shoulder is getting stiff. Hanging from the harness, I find a handhold where the right edge of the crack curls inward. Look at my feet through the NODs. There's a foothold for my left foot, not my right. I cross my ankles and find friction between the sole of my right trainer and the rock.

Alright, I can unload the Prusik. Time remains a factor, so I climb. Retrace my route to the anchor. When I get there, I test it. Both pitons held. Neither is loose. I was careless about falling rock. The anchor saved my life.

I set off across the ledge a second time. Every ten feet, I hammer pitons into the face. All my senses are hyper-sensitized to signs of falling rock. The pains in my muscles persist. Rather than localized, exquisite agony, they blur into a diffuse ache. My shoulder regains mobility. The traverse is not as physically demanding as the climb. Soon enough, the work will get harder.

The chimney is everything I expected. Its width is consistent all the way to the monastery. Somewhat narrower than the span of a man's spread arms. Had the chimney been tighter than that, I wouldn't have considered it. Many chimneys won't fit a man unless he takes off his pack.

With two pitons, I build my third and final anchor at the base of the chimney. The second bag is still heavy with a hundred and fifty feet of rope. The remaining fifty feet stretch across the traverse. I draw the Cold Steel OSS from its sheath and cut off the fifty-foot tail. Zip the bag shut, loop the strap around the outside of my new anchor.

I return my knife to its sheath, unzip the third bag. Take the fresh rope and tie the end into the anchor. Fasten the rope to my harness with a Prusik, prepare to ascend.

Step across the chimney, brace one foot and one hand against each wall. This is a friction game, a pressure game. So long as I apply pressure against the walls, I can maintain the stance. I lift one foot and move it up, applying pressure on the remaining three points. When that foot is set against the stone, I lift the other foot. Once both feet are planted, and my knees are bent, I release my hands, straighten my legs, and advance with my palms along the chimney.

When I find a particularly good crack, I insert a piton in one wall. One-handed, I hammer it in. After my fall, I'm taking no chances. It's painstaking work, but I make steady progress. Thirty feet from the clifftop, I pound in a piton and clip the hammer to my belt.

It's not likely anyone on the clifftop heard me when I was far below. From here on, the risks of detection increase. A sixty-foot fall will wipe me out, but so will a pirate with a USP standing at the top.

With ten feet to go, I search for hand and footholds on the left wall. Keep going. Three feet from the top, I find a diagonal seam. I grasp it with my left hand. My feet are braced against the wall, supported by pressure. I use my NODs. Looking through the right tube, I examine the wall around my left foot.

One skinny foothold. I plant my left trainer on it, then grab the seam with my right hand. My body's twisted up, supported on three points. I straighten, shift my right foot to the left wall. My arms and left leg quake with fatigue. I scrabble around with the toe of my right trainer, hunting for purchase.

I find it. A tiny ridge raised by a fraction of an inch. I rest my right toe on the feature. Shift as much weight as I can manage away from my left leg. The respite from pain is delicious. Strength pours into me.

Three rotten feet to the lip of the chimney and the clifftop beyond. If I can grasp the lip with my hands, I can shift my feet onto the seam below. I take deep breaths, rehearse the move in my mind's eye.

Reach up, grasp the lip with my right hand. Squeeze like I want to punch finger-holes into the rock. Contort my body, throw weight on my left leg and lift my right foot high. Scrape the wall with the edge of my shoe. Try again, dig my heel into the seam. My leg is almost straight, just a slight bend at the knee. I have it. My arms and right leg unload my left.

I release the seam with my left hand and grab the lip. Now I have two hands on solid rock at the top of the cliff. With the extension of my arm, my left foot comes off its step naturally. It finds no purchase, but I have three other points supporting my weight.

Take a deep breath, grunt. With one mighty heave, I throw my right leg over the lip. Pull as hard as I can with my arms, muscles cording like steel cables. Steel cables don't burn with pain, and the agony that comes with the explosive contraction of those sinews sears my brain. My trunk rolls over the top, drags my left leg along. Before I know it, I'm lying on my back on the clifftop. My body's weight crushes the empty rope bag beneath me.

Above me, Koitída Sofias obscures the stars.

THE SOUTH WALL of the monastery is flush to the cliff face. The stone and mortar walls are separated from the cliff by six inches of friable rock. I was right to ascend via the chimney. Had I continued along the first vertical crack, I would have had little space to collect myself at the top. Penetration of the building would have been more difficult.

The top of the chimney is a narrow rock shelf, three feet wide. The shelf abuts the stone wall of Koitída Sofias. A homeless man in a sleeping bag has more room on the sidewalk than I have to work with.

Crucially, this junction between cliff and monastery prevents the pirates from posting guards. No sentry is going to stand all night on a ledge three feet deep and seven feet long. He isn't going to walk along the six inches of rock that separate the monastery from a four-hundred-foot plunge.

Problem is, neither am I. The south wall of the monastery is a hundred yards wide. It takes up the whole promontory.

I'm not done climbing.

Magellan Voyager, my go-to application for online reconnaissance, has no detail on the interior of Koitída Sofias. Magellan combines maps, photographs and satellite imagery to provide users with a virtual 3D experience of any location on the planet. It is naturally limited by the data and photographs available open source. There isn't much available on the monastery.

That means I have to rely on the photographs I took of the exterior, and satellite imagery.

Medieval monasteries were religious forts. Monks were the guardians of libraries, jewelry, and priceless religious artifacts. They built their monasteries in secluded locations that were difficult to approach. The structures were difficult to breach.

The outer wall of Koitída Sofias is stone and mortar, fifteen feet high. That wall surrounds the main building, one hundred yards wide and twenty yards deep. It overlooks the Mediterranean and the south face. There are two more large, rectangular buildings on the promontory, one on each side. They have been grafted onto the south structure to form a U shape. They are both constructed with stone and mortar walls contiguous with that of the main building. In fact, the monks extended that wall so that it completely enclosed a number of subsidiary buildings on the north side of the compound. They added a stout gate, to complete a defensive perimeter against attack from the north.

Between the two wings of the U sits the compound's major feature. The *katholikón*—the monastery's Byzantine church—is large for such an isolated monastery. It is testimony to the wealth of the order, because the grand structure was built for the monks, not the people. It could *not* have been built for the people. Koitída Sofias is so isolated that even today there is no one around.

The interior must be grand, because the order would not have built such a large structure to house an empty *katholikón*. No, it had to be brilliant in every respect, to make the monks feel close to God. The structure is cruciform, with a long nave and stubby transepts. There appear to be two domes, one above the center of the nave, and one above the sanctuary.

No expense was spared.

Carefully, I get to my feet and stretch. I needn't have worried about being heard. There are no sentries about. I scan the wall through the right tube of my NODs. It's not as impregnable as the monks thought. The stones are like over-sized bricks with convex faces, held together by mortar. They provide abundant hand and footholds. Above the wall, the monastery is built of wood. There are three stories, long rows of windows and balconies.

I scan the balconies for any sign of sentries, but there is no one to be seen. That doesn't matter—they could be on watch behind the windows.

Like a common second-story man, I view those balconies as a vulnerability. There are galvanized metal drains that run from the eaves of the roof to the cliff. The eaves are both functional and ornamental. They conceal gutters that run around the edge of the roof, channeling runoff rainwater to the drains. The eaves have also been cut in an attractive ornamental trim.

The drains are purely functional. Painted brown, they have been fastened to the wooden walls by metal strips and thick screws. They run vertically between windows, past the balconies.

There *are* people up there. Our Sea Hawk was detected hovering over Bie Eirini. A warning was transmitted to Ésperos. But Koitída Sofias is a big place for two dozen pirates to rattle around in.

Not sure I'll trust the drains to hold my weight, but we'll see. It all depends on how sturdy the screws are.

I pound a piton into the base of the wall. Undo my

climbing rope and secure it to the anchor. Then I shrug off the rope bag and take off my climbing harness. It feels good to be free of all that weight. I drain half my canteen in one long gulp, then return it to the case on my pistol belt.

Hands on hips, I exhale and study the wall. The monastery looks completely dark. Fifteen feet of stone and mortar, then the first story. There's a balcony about ten feet above me and to the left. The balcony has a wooden safety rail. There are two windows and a door behind it. The second story is twelve feet above the first, the third story twelve feet above that. There are other balconies, and long rows of dark windows stretch between them.

My priority is to find Stein, and I need to take an organized approach. I'll start at the top and work my way down. I step to the drain and seize the metal pipe in both hands. Lean back and set my weight against it. The screws withstand the first assault. I plant the soles of my feet on either side and try again. The screws hold.

I free-climb to the third story. Reach over with my left hand and grab the rail of the balcony. Let go of the drain with my right hand, transfer my grip to the rail.

For a second, I dangle in space, hanging by my arms. I look into a four-hundred-and-forty-foot abyss. Do a straightforward pull-up, throw my right leg over the rail, and roll onto the balcony. Land catlike on my toes.

Step to the door, try the handle. It's locked. Why would anybody lock a door to a balcony that overlooks a four-hundred-and-forty-foot drop? Don't the idiots know they're safe?

My Benchmade multi-tool has a utility knife. I'm not going to use my Cold Steel on this lock. I set my shoulder against the door. It's loose enough that my weight creates a

small seam between the door and the jamb. I push the point
of the knife into the space, search for the latch bolt.

Can't quite get it. I wiggle the knife around. Need to get
the blade parallel to the face plate and the point onto the bolt.
I lean on the knife, use the doorjamb as the fulcrum of a lever.
There's a distinct crack as the doorjamb splinters. The blade
crushes the wood flat. The point rides high on the latch bolt's
surface. I push hard and twist. I'm rewarded by a click as the
latch disengages. Under my weight, the door springs open.

I step into the room. In the dark, I fold my multi-tool
shut and squeeze it back into my pocket. Reach up to my
NODs, take the left tube off close-focus. Now I'm back to
binocular vision, with normal depth perception. My brain
processes the nature and quality of the sensory data, adapts
seamlessly.

Reach down, unsnap my holster. The Mark 23 is loaded
and decocked.

The interior of the monastery is uncharted territory. The
room I'm standing in is thirty feet wide on the side that faces
the ocean. Twenty-five feet deep. There's a long wooden
table in the center, running parallel to the windows. The
other three sides of the room are covered with bookshelves.
The room is corner-fed. There's a single interior door opposite the balcony.

The air is cool, laced with a musty smell. I recognize it—
books. It's a reading room. The place is a library. The shelves
rise, floor to ceiling. Stepladders slide on rails fixed at their
base.

"Sarkis?"

The voice from the hall startles me. A man is
approaching from the corridor outside. He must have heard

me break in. That was always a risk, but there's no accounting for dumb luck. Now he thinks I'm Sarkis—whoever *he* is. All I need is for Sarkis to hear this guy call his name.

I step around the table. The man pushes the door open, enters the room. I can see him clearly with my night vision, he sees nothing but a shadow stepping in front of him. I palm strike him under the chin and heel his head back. Spear him with four fingers in his exposed throat.

The man chokes. I throw him face down on the floor, drop my knee on the small of his back. Reach around and grab his jaw with my right hand, cup his grizzled chin in my palm. My fingers bury themselves in his cheek. My left hand goes to the back of his neck. I pull his head back with my right hand, shove his neck forward with my left. Helpless, he chokes and flails. With a sharp twist, I break his neck. There's a crunch as his vertebrae separate.

When you break a man's neck, it doesn't wobble around like a wet noodle. The skull, especially if he's a strong man, is supported by muscles and sturdy connective tissue. What you get is this ugly grinding sensation when the separated segments of the spinal column rub against each other. Your brain is a strange thing. You think you *hear* the grinding, but you don't. What your brain is doing is *imagining* the sound of grinding, based on the *sensation* of grinding. You feel your enemy's disarticulated bones rub together, and your brain adds the soundtrack.

I get to my feet, open the door to the balcony. Grab the corpse by the wrists and drag it outside. He's wearing a USP holstered at his right hip. Never drew it. That means he wasn't expecting a threat. He was looking for his friend.

Didn't hear me break in. I caught him completely by surprise.

I stand the dead man up, shove him against the rail, and pitch him over the side. I watch the body tumble head over heels, a shadow in the moonlight. It scrapes against the cliff face once. Plunges to the beach and lands with a dull thud. At a distance of four hundred feet, I barely hear it.

Turn around, go back inside.

The dead man and his friend, Sarkis, were wandering around the dark monastery. Doing what? They weren't looking for me, that's for certain.

I need to find Stein.

"Miklos!" a man shouts. I hear running footsteps in the hall.

Now the man I killed has a name. I jerk open the reading room's door, look into the hall. Keep most of my body behind cover. No way I'm going to jump out and get shot. A girl is running toward me, her features shockingly clear in the green glow of the NODs.

It's Hecate. She screams when she sees a shadowy figure with glowing green eyes. Sarkis is chasing her along the corridor. When he sees me, he's as shocked as she is. It's pretty obvious I'm not Miklos. I'm a threatening creature, a demon. He reaches for his USP.

I extend an arm, grab Hecate as she tries to get past.

"Get down," I tell her. I draw my Mark 23.

Drag Hecate to the floor. She struggles, but I throw my weight on her.

Pop, pop, pop.

Sarkis's 9mm USP sounds like a rapid-fire popgun.

Muzzle flashes from the pistol light the corridor like bolts of lightning. I pin Hecate to the floor with my weight, control her with my left arm. The pirate's shots go high—he never had a clear look at me in the dark.

Extend the Mark 23, point-shoot him twice. The first round puts him down hard. He's falling by the time the second round enters under his chin and blows the top of his head off. In the electric green glow of the NODs, the blood spray is a black halo.

Hecate is pummeling me with her fists. "Let me go!"

"Be quiet," I say. "It's Breed."

"Breed?"

I didn't stutter, so I don't bother to respond. Instead, I put my left hand flat on her head and push it against the hard floor. "Stay down," I say.

Get up, walk to Sarkis. He's on his back, arms outflung. I step on his right wrist, relieve him of the USP. The top of his skull is gone, and the splatter has formed a black cone for six feet behind him. He won't require a third round.

I step over to Hecate and help her to her feet. She and the pirates were working with night vision they developed in the dark corridor. My NODs give me a decisive advantage.

"Do you know this place?" I ask.

"No. What are you doing here?"

"Later. Where are Stein and your father?"

"In the *katholikón*. Drakos is holding them prisoner."

"How many more are after you?"

"Four or five."

"Come on."

There are doorways on either side of the corridor. This is a library floor. Reading rooms covering different subjects. There must be stairways at either end. We're on the third wooden story, so there must be two more wooden stories below us, and a ground floor behind the fifteen-foot stone wall. Most structures have basements. If Koitída Sofias has a basement, it would have to be cut into the rock of the cliff.

I try to remember the satellite photographs. The two buildings on either side have been grafted onto this structure. The floors are probably linked. The *katholikón* in the middle is separate from the rest.

Does it make sense for Drakos to hold prisoners in the church? There are no cloisters between the church and the other buildings. The monks would have had to walk outdoors to the church in bad weather.

I take Hecate by the hand and we hurry to the end of the corridor. As I expected, a staircase leads to the other floors. I'm not going to let the pirates trap us on the top-most story. The staircase is dimly lit by 25-watt tungsten bulbs in wire cages on the ceiling of each landing. I flip up my NODs. Lead Hecate into the stairwell and descend to the first story. Two wooden stories above us, the ground floor below, behind its stone wall. Maybe a basement.

Wherever the other pirates are, they may have heard our gunshots. Hearing gunshots is one thing, localizing them is another. They won't know where the fight took place. By picking a random story, I'm making it harder for them. They'll have to organize a search. Start at the bottom and work up, or start at the top and work down. Cover the main building and the wings. That will buy time for me to get a story out of Hecate.

Corridors are deathtraps. Operators avoid them like the plague. All it takes is one bad guy to point an automatic rifle into a corridor and hose it down. He doesn't even have to aim. Just move his muzzle in a little circle and hold the trigger down. A unit creeping along the corridor will be cut to pieces.

I push Hecate against the wall of the stairwell. There's a light switch on the wall. I flick the switch, plunge the stairwell into darkness.

Reflexively, Hecate grips my arm.

There's a good chance the space on the other side of that door is dark. I'm not going to open the door and let myself be silhouetted against a lighted stairwell. I don't see any light under the door. Flip my NODs down, open the door a crack.

I study the length of the corridor, find it empty. Take Hecate by the hand and go inside. Close the door behind us.

The first story looks like a duplicate of the third. As such, it suits my purpose for a temporary hideout. I don't want to go into a room in the middle of the corridor. There's too far to go if we're discovered. I push open a door on the right and step into a large reading room like the one two stories above. The walls are lined with bookshelves, and reading tables are set up in the center of the room.

The wooden bookshelves have hinged glass doors with rubber seals. The bookshelves are equipped with steel locks. I wonder how many of these volumes have been hand-copied and hand-bound. Not all, but a significant number. The Koitída Sofías library must be worth a fortune.

The ocean and night sky are visible, and moonlight streams through the windows. I flip up my NODs and allow my eyes to adjust. Find a comfortable seat facing the door, guide Hecate to a seat next to me. She sits down, and I release her hand.

"We'll be safe here for a while," I tell her, "but we can't afford to be careless. They'll come after those two, but will have to get organized first."

"You found your needle," Hecate says.

"I did. It's in Bie Eirini, the cove at the foot of this monastery."

"I know."

"How do you know?"

"It's something of a story."

"We don't have much time," I say. "Tell me."

18

THE FOURTH DAY – EARLY MORNING,
KOITÍDA SOFIAS

I lean back, try to relax. Stretch out my right arm on the table, point the Mark 23 at the door. This won't work. Exhausted muscles only stiffen when you stop moving. All the lactic acid produced when you exercise is flushed away in your blood. When you rest, your heart rate slows, and your blood carries away less acid. The rest sits in your muscles and you get stiff.

Was it just two nights ago I boarded the *Goliath*? Events have raced forward with a life of their own. I have most of the pieces of the puzzle, but not all of them. The most important ones elude me. Hecate may have them.

Hecate turns in her chair, sits close to me with her elbows on her knees. It's an intimate posture. Her scent reminds me of our night together. In a low voice, she tells me what happened.

HECATE WATCHED the Sea Hawk lift from the beach. As it turned in place, she saw Breed staring at her from the open door. She was overcome with warmth and waved to him. He smiled and waved back. The helicopter turned in place, pitched slightly nose-down, and flew toward Crete.

Like a wave of cold brine, a feeling of dread washed over her. Greeks are a superstitious people. Despite her western education, Hecate would never laugh at the casting of an evil eye. She told herself Breed could handle whatever trouble he might encounter.

Hecate turned and walked back to the stone steps that led to Ésperos. She liked Breed, and not only because he satisfied her appetite. He wasn't afraid of women and was straightforward about what he wanted. She could tell he treated women well. This was unusual nowadays, when so many men tried to curry favor by espousing values they thought women would appreciate.

She picked up her book from the deck chair. Closed it on her finger to mark her place, then stepped into the living room. Stein was sitting at a table, tapping on her laptop. "Breed has gone in the helicopter," Hecate told her.

It was a silly thing to say. Stein already knew Breed had gone, but Hecate wanted to make small talk with the American woman who had slept with her father.

"Thank you." Stein didn't look up from her laptop. She was upset with Hecate for sleeping with Breed.

Hecate could tell Breed and Stein were attracted to each other, but they had a professional relationship to worry about. Stein was conflicted. A successful western woman, she was used to men seeking her favor. Confused when they resented her for granting it. Breed was the kind of man she wanted, yet the kind she was not supposed to want.

Hecate made peace with her own conflicts. She was a Greek girl, though she spent many years studying in England. Her father wanted her to be comfortable in western ways. In that, he was wise. As a Greek, Hecate was more of the east than the west. It was the rare westerner who understood Greek culture and temperament.

Greeks don't smile much around strangers. Men and women are not openly amorous, and western flirtation is not readily understood.

Hecate understood the Greek ways, but grew up with the fast life of an English university town. She learned to exist in the space between east and west. Being Athanasios Kyrios's daughter helped. People in her social circle, her *parea*, who might otherwise have disapproved, accepted her behavior because "She's Thanos's girl."

Breed was refreshing because Hecate intimidated many Greek men.

In her room, Hecate found the sheets changed, her bed made. The Kyrios servants were efficient. She dressed in her day clothes and sat by the window, where she could enjoy the breeze. Opened her book and began to read. She did not want to share space with Stein.

That afternoon, a maid came to her door. "Ms Kyrios, your father wants you to join him downstairs."

"Why?"

"He and Mr Drakos are taking his guests to Koitída Sofias. He wants you to go."

Hecate was intrigued. Drakos had purchased the medieval monastery at Bie Eirini. She had seen it from the air and ocean, but had never been inside. Hecate put her book aside and went downstairs.

Her father, Drakos, and Harding-James were standing

around Stein. The Deputy Director was sliding her laptop into her briefcase.

"Are you sure I can use my laptop from your yacht?" Stein asked Kyrios.

"Of course. *Grigoro Fidi* has full satellite connectivity."

"I should stay here," Stein said. "In case Breed tries to reach me."

"There is nothing you can do here that you cannot do on the *Fidi*," Kyrios said. "Come see the waters where your quarry is supposed to have sailed. We might even run into her."

They walked onto the terrace. Inhaled the fresh, salty air. The sea and sky were blue as far as the eye could see. A motor launch was carrying six men of Drakos's security detail to the *Grigoro Fidi*.

Drakos had joined them on sails before. There was nothing particularly sinister about the bearded Greek, although Hecate considered the man crude. While Kyrios was comfortable with people of all classes and walks of life, Hecate looked askance at the Drakos family history. Soon, Hecate would take over Kyrios Shipping. She wondered what Drakos would be like to deal with.

Drakos treated Hecate like a niece. When he visited, he would bring her little gifts. A box of *bougatsa* made by his wife, or a bottle of wine. Hecate was appreciative and polite, but she never allowed him to penetrate her careful reserve.

The little group walked onto the pier to meet the launch. The afternoon sun beat warm on Hecate's face. The sea breeze ruffled her skirt. Hecate watched her father take Stein's hand and help her into the boat.

When they reached the *Grigoro Fidi*, Hecate found the yacht's deck shivering with the power of its four turbine engines. It was unusual for *Fidi* to run on four. The *Fidi* was a powerful vessel, and it easily made thirty knots on two screws. Kyrios shouted instructions to sailors and the yacht pulled away from Ésperos.

They went inside the saloon, and Kyrios showed Stein to a comfortable seat in front of a table. Invited her to plug in her laptop.

"How do I connect to the internet?" Stein asked.

"That, I cannot help you with." Kyrios laughed. "Hecate will show you."

Kyrios led Drakos and Harding-James onto the bridge. Hecate sat next to Stein and showed her how to connect to the *Fidi*'s network. It was an easy exercise. No more difficult than connecting from a restaurant or coffee shop in downtown London or Athens. The yacht's satellite connectivity was seamless.

"Well, that was simple." Stein smiled at Hecate. "Thank you so much."

To smile is to deceive.

"It's my pleasure, Ms Stein. If there is anything else I can do to help, let me know."

The vibration under Hecate's feet increased. *Fidi* was running on four screws. The sea was smooth as glass, and the yacht was cutting through it like a high-speed patrol boat. The saloon was far forward and insulated from the engine noise. Hecate could hear the hiss of water along the sides of the *Fidi*'s hull. She was travelling at close to fifty knots.

Kyrios entered the saloon from the bridge.

"Why are we in a hurry?" Hecate asked in Greek.

"This must be a quick outing. We want to return to Ésperos by dusk."

Sensible enough. It would not take long for Drakos to show them Koitída Sofías.

Kyrios turned to Stein. "Are you sure you do not want to join us on the bridge?"

"I'm fine, Thanos. I have to keep working. Anything I can do to narrow Breed's search will help."

"Of course, but you must join us when we approach the monastery. I insist."

"Alright, let me know."

"I will send someone to bring you a drink. Come, Hecate."

Hecate followed her father onto the bridge. The captain and helmsman were navigating the *Grigoro Fidi* at high speed. Kyrios continued to climb the companionway to the navigation bridge.

The cool sea wind blew Hecate's hair back. She knew that it would keep her from feeling the heat of the sun. It would not take long to develop sunburn. There were two sailors, one on each side. Drakos and Harding-James were leaning against the front rail.

A large container vessel passed on the *Fidi*'s port side, a mile distant. Hecate noticed that most of the traffic was commercial. The *Fidi* was speeding across the Mediterranean, south of Karpathos and Kasos. It was avoiding the littoral waters to the north. The Aegean had more pleasure traffic, and the *Fidi* would have to slow down.

"We shall be at the monastery in an hour," Kyrios said.

Hecate leaned on the rail, turned to Drakos. "How did you come to buy the monastery?"

Drakos laughed. "Technically, I have not bought it. I have leased it from the order—for one hundred years."

"Leased?"

"They would not sell. Too much history, no place to store their valuables, their libraries. So they inventoried every item and leased it to me on the condition that I protect the integrity of the site."

"Is it as grand as Metéora?" Hecate had once visited the soaring complex of monasteries built on thousand-foot-high sandstone pillars in Thessaly. The monks hand-climbed the pillars, then roped up supplies with which to build the monasteries.

"No." Drakos shook his head. "Nothing can compare to Metéora, except Mount Athos. But Koitída Sofias was built in a beautiful, isolated place. Perfect for contemplation and study. Their libraries are vast. The *katholikón* contains mosaics and icons of inestimable value."

"Are they not afraid of theft?"

"The isolation of Koitída Sofias is protection enough. But they had a security force on the premises. When I took over, I replaced them with my own."

Hecate looked back along the *Grigoro Fidi*'s turbulent wake. One of Drakos's security detail was standing on the boat deck, speaking with a member of the *Fidi*'s crew.

"I'm going below." Hecate turned and stepped to the companionway. "It is too windy here."

"Let us go keep Anya company," Kyrios said.

On the bridge, Hecate noticed that two of Drakos's security team had joined the captain and helmsman. They were looking out the windows. The *Fidi* had passed the blue-gray mass of Kasos, receding on their right.

They found Stein sipping a glass of wine. Her laptop, survival radio, and a pad of paper were spread on the table.

Kyrios went to the bar. "Have you found any sign of the *Medusa*, Anya?"

"No." Stein exhaled and leaned back in her chair. "Whoever took her has exercised tight control over their communications."

Drakos folded his arms over his barrel chest. "The earth has swallowed her up."

"I wouldn't go that far." Stein furrowed her brow, glanced at her survival radio. "Breed is doing the visual search, and he hasn't called in."

"What would you like?" Kyrios asked Hecate.

"Ouzo and ice."

Kyrios poured a glass of ouzo. Fished a single ice cube from an insulated pot, dropped it in. Hecate liked to watch the drink cloud as it chilled.

Stein's survival radio lit up and buzzed.

"It's Breed." Stein reached for the device.

"Don't touch it, Stein."

Stein froze. Four pairs of eyes swung toward Drakos. They focused, not on him, but on his H&K USP Compact. The stubby pistol with its four-inch barrel seemed buried in his giant paw. Its muzzle was fixed on Stein.

"Drakos?" Kyrios froze in the middle of pouring a drink.

"Be silent, Thanos. We will be at Koitída Sofias soon. If she is not foolish, Stein may learn what happened to the *Medusa*."

One of Drakos's security detail stepped into the saloon. The man carried a USP in his right hand. Hecate remembered two bodyguards on the bridge. That meant one remained with the captain and helmsman. There were four others aboard.

"Stand up, Stein. Keep both of your hands in view."

Stein rose, hands spread.

Drakos was pleased with himself. He addressed his

bodyguard in English. "Miklos, the lady was kind enough to show us her weapon last night. It is in a holster at her hip. Relieve her of it."

The man raised the flap of stein's jacket and pulled her SIG from its holster. Stepped back and slipped it into his waistband.

"May I sit down?" Stein asked.

"By all means." Drakos stepped to the table, picked up Stein's survival radio, and pocketed it. As she sat, he reached over and slapped her laptop shut. "Let's keep that keyboard out of reach as well."

"Apparently, the Drakos family still engages in hijacking," Stein said.

"It is not a major line of business, but this opportunity was too good to pass up." Drakos looked around the saloon. "Everyone sit down. We shall relax until we arrive at the monastery. It will not be long. Kyrios, let me have a Cutty Sark and soda. Ash, what will you have?"

"Same."

Drakos nodded. "Hecate, please bring the drinks to us. Enjoy your ouzo."

"The *Goliath* was your ship." Stein was determined to learn as much as she could.

"Yes. Among others. My fleet is not as large as Kyrios Shipping, but I have enough. After all, once Thanos's father decided not to accept our cargoes, we had to do something."

"Of course, you had to acquire transponder spoofing technology."

"Acquire? We are at the forefront of development. The techniques we used to take the *Medusa* were not difficult."

"You *did* leave a trail."

"It's not yet possible to completely avoid leaving traces.

You found the general direction, but not *Medusa*'s exact location."

Drakos accepted his whiskey and soda from Hecate and sank into a leather chair. He held the drink in his left hand, the pistol in his right. Miklos stood by the door to the bridge, covering the saloon.

"Look around you, Stein. We are at the mouth of the Aegean. The *Medusa* had to pass through here. Then, one black night, she encountered *Goliath*. A medical case that had to be transferred immediately and carried north. A launch was sent over, a boarding ladder was lowered. The rest was easy."

"There was a security force aboard."

"They were caught unaware. This isn't the horn of Africa, Stein. There are no pirates in these waters. The security detail expected an uneventful cruise and easy money."

Drakos's other bodyguard leaned into the saloon. "We have arrived," he said.

Hecate could feel the vibration easing under her flat-soled shoes. The *Grigoro Fidi* was running on two engines, not four. The two that were running had been throttled back.

"Let's go to the navigation bridge." Drakos got to his feet and gestured with his USP.

Miklos preceded the group and climbed the companion-way. Drakos brought up the rear.

Hecate loved the Greek islands. The views were breath-taking, and this was the most striking view on Crete. The *Grigoro Fidi* was approaching Bie Eirini on a perfectly calm ocean. Blue water, blue sky, black cliffs. The Koitída Sofias was like a fortress, perched on the promontory.

The coast on either side of the monastery was uninhab-

ited. The monks couldn't have picked a more isolated place
to build their fortress of contemplation.

"What are you doing?" Kyrios put his hand on Drakos's
arm.

"You will see."

The *Grigoro Fidi* turned until its bow was pointing south
and its stern was to the cove.

"Come." Drakos descended the companionway. Led the
group through the saloon and onto the after well deck. They
joined two crewmen and two of Drakos's bodyguards. One of
the crewmen held a line-of-sight radio in his hand. He was
giving directions to the helmsman.

"Why are you *reversing* into the cove?" Stein couldn't hide
her surprise.

Drakos smiled.

With infinite care, the crew of the *Grigoro Fidi* backed the
yacht into Bie Eirini. There was more than enough room. A
hundred and twenty feet long, the yacht had a beam of
twenty-five feet. The mouth of the cove was a hundred feet
wide.

Hecate felt a chill as the *Fidi* edged into the shadow of
the cliffs. The rock faces stretched from the ocean to the sky.
She couldn't understand what Drakos and the crew were
doing. There was no place in the cove to tie up. There was
nothing around them but stone and water.

Next to her, Stein stiffened. Hecate turned to see what
she was staring at.

The black face of the cliff was splitting open. Like a stage
curtain, heavy canvas shutters were being drawn aside by
powerful electric motors. The shutters were painted with
alternating black and gray vertical strokes to make them
look like a cracked limestone surface. Fully open, the shut-

ters revealed a sea cave, a hundred feet wide and fifty feet high. The interior was brightly lit. The crewman with the radio barked instructions, and the *Fidi* crept backward into the cave.

"But where is *Medusa*?" Stein craned her neck to see into the corners of the cave.

Hecate could see that the cave was over two hundred feet deep, and a broad wooden dock had been built on three sides. Like many caves, it was part of a cavern system. They were entering the cave from the ocean side, but there were openings to at least three other chambers at the far end. It was likely the cave had been cut a thousand years ago by an underground stream that dried up over the centuries.

Stein turned to Drakos. "Where is it? Where's *Medusa*?"

"We passed over her."

Realization dawned on Stein. "The *ocean* swallowed her up."

"Yes. She's out there, two hundred yards off Bie Eirini. We brought her in at night, opened the sea cocks, and down she went. On an even keel. We had two fishing trawlers waiting, replete with fishing nets. But the nets were modified with camouflage panels. The trawlers laid the nets over the *Medusa* and deployed divers to secure the nets in place."

"Where is the crew?" Kyrios asked.

"We set them on a deserted island, west of Kasos. There are thousands such. No radio, no flares, plenty of water. They will be found in a few days."

"Look, there's the gold," Harding-James said.

Hecate and Stein followed the Englishman's pointing finger. There, set on the dock at the far end of the cave, were sixty wooden pallets, each two feet square, carrying gold in transparent plastic cases. Each pallet half a ton, thirty tons in total. Two billion dollars.

The length of the *Grigoro Fidi* was inside the cave. Electric motors whined, closed the camouflage shutters. The helmsman alternated the port and starboard screws in short bursts to back the *Fidi* to the dock.

Electric cranes sat on the docks. Hecate counted four. Two were on either side of the pallets. One was parked at the opening of one of the three secondary chambers. The fourth crane was on the dock to *Fidi's* starboard. There, Hecate could see two large sleds. They sat on runners like catamarans, but each stood no more than three feet high. Each had two electric motors and two screws, protected by plastic shrouds. Each sled's bow had space for two pilots. Hecate realized they were underwater sleighs, used to transport the gold from the *Medusa* to the hidden dock.

Next to the sea sleighs stood an industrial-capacity filling station. It was equipped with multiple compressors with which to charge scuba tanks. A large rectangular space was occupied by dozens of bottles. The pirates had divers working 24/7 since the *Medusa* had been scuttled. It was a major diving operation. Bottles had to be kept filled, and each diver's time underwater and number of dives per day had to be monitored.

There were fifteen men on the dock. Several carried submachine guns. One man shouted to the sailor on the fantail in Greek, "Do you have a gangplank aboard?"

"Yes. Starboard."

"Lower it. We will help you."

The crewman spoke into his radio. Fore and aft, ropes were thrown across to the *Fidi*. The yacht was tied to the dock. The crew lowered a gangplank with safety rails.

"Come." Drakos led the way to the gangplank.

"Where are we going?" Hecate asked.

"You wanted to see Koitída Sofias."

DRAKOS GAVE orders for the gold to be transferred to the *Grigoro Fidi*. The men on the dock maneuvered a crane into place. Workers and crew gathered on the dock and at the fantail of the yacht. They began to swing pallets aboard.

The yacht was not designed to carry cargo. It was impossible to stack the pallets on the well deck. Rather, the pallets were fitted next to each other like a mosaic. The transfer was an incredibly difficult task. Hecate wondered why they did not transfer the gold to a proper freighter under cover of darkness. A geared freighter with its own booms and dedicated cargo holds was much more appropriate.

Drakos and his six bodyguards took Hecate and the others into one of the three chambers that extended into the cliff. The chamber was used for storage space. There were racks of diving gear. Wet suits, face masks, weight belts, flippers.

To her surprise, Drakos motioned them to a stone staircase on the left. Hewn out of the limestone. The staircase was high and wide, and rose in a counter-clockwise direction. That was strange. Medieval staircases in castles rose in a clockwise direction. That made it difficult for a right-handed attacker coming up the stairs to swing his sword.

Hecate led the way up the stairs, followed by Stein and Drakos. Then came Harding-James, her father, and the bodyguards. The bodyguards were armed with pistols and submachine guns. As she struggled up the steps, she realized why the staircase rose counter-clockwise. It was meant to make it easy for a defender at the foot of the stairs to defend against attackers coming *down*.

The staircase and cave were an escape route. If attackers seized the monastery, the monks and their defenders would flee *down* the steps to waiting boats.

Electric bulbs had been strung at regular intervals along the staircase. It was a simple series. The wire was hung from hooks screwed into the limestone ceiling. The air was cold and the stone was damp. Hecate was not given to claustrophobia, but the walls closed in on her. She wanted the climb to be over.

"Pace yourself." Drakos's voice echoed in the staircase.

"How far is it?" Hecate was gasping. Behind her, she could hear Drakos breathing hard. Stein didn't seem to be tiring at all.

"There are over a thousand steps," Drakos said. "Always, I lose count."

Hecate reached the top, found herself face-to-face with a wooden panel. She placed her hands flat on the smooth, varnished wood. "I'm at the top," she said.

"Push on the panel," Drakos said. "Wait for us on the other side."

Hecate pushed and the panel swung open easily. She found herself in a small chapel. This was the sacristy, or Chapel of Oblation. It was decorated with icons that stared down at a wide Table of Oblation, where offerings were prepared. The table was covered with richly embroidered coverings. Set on the table were the vessels used in the preparation of the Sacrament of the Holy Eucharist. The vestments, cups and candelabra were orthodox in design. The metalwork was encrusted in jewels.

There was a gold *crux orthodoxa*—an Eastern Orthodox Cross—hung on one wall. A vertical post, a long cross-piece two-thirds of the way up, a shorter cross-piece above that, and a diagonal cross-piece below. Hecate was familiar with the symbolism. The short bar on top represented the scroll above the crucified savior. The diagonal bar below represented the two thieves crucified on either side of Christ. The man on Christ's left repented and was saved. The bar on his side has been elevated to heaven. The man on the savior's right rejected his love, so that side of the bar points to hell.

Stein joined Hecate in the sacristy. She looked as fresh as she had at Ésperos. Drakos leaned against one wall and waited to catch his breath. They waited a long time for Harding-James and the others to join them. The entire group halted on the narrow stairs when the heavy Englishman stopped to rest.

"Here." Drakos opened the sacristy door and the group found themselves in the *katholikón*. They stood behind the high altar, in the ambulatory. On the other side of the high altar, opposite the sacristy, was the Diakonnikon, or vestry. This was a room reserved for sacred vessels, books and vestments. It was called the Diakonnikon because the church Deacons were responsible for these items. It corresponds to what Catholics or Protestants consider the sacristies of their churches.

The *katholikón* was beautiful. Here, in a monastery built to house a hundred monks, the order built a church with space for five hundred. Hecate stood behind the high altar and stared at the icons and stained glass. She turned in place, dazzled. The *katholikón* was in the center of Koitída Sofias, at the top of the cliff. The sun shone brightly through the windows. Electric blue and blazing red colors were cast on the floor, the altar, and the faces of the guests. Hecate glanced at Stein, saw the young woman's face painted blue, red and gold. Saw her eyes light up with wonder.

Drakos stepped around the magnificent high altar. The space around the altar was demarcated by polished wooden rails. This was the sanctuary, the most holy part of the *katholikón*. Four sets of stacidia, high-backed wooden chairs, were arranged on either side. The bearded Greek stepped over to one of the chairs, threw himself down, and motioned to Hecate and Stein to sit across from him.

"Are you impressed?" Drakos asked Hecate.

"It's beautiful." Hecate studied their host. She had known Drakos all her life. Never had she seen him like this.

Harding-James collapsed on a chair next to Hecate. Kyrios sat next to Stein. The stacidia were uncomfortable. Hecate studied the enclosed space of the sanctuary. It was grand, but it was separated from the nave of the church by a tall wooden screen, the iconostasis. Hecate knew the *katholikón* would be at least three times the size of the sanctuary in which they found themselves.

The iconostasis was meant to symbolize the separation of the congregation from the holiest of holy places. It symbolized that the sanctuary could only be reached through striving. In the center of the iconostasis was the gilded Royal Gate. On either side of the Royal Gate were two deacon's doors through which clergy passed into the sanctuary in the course of ceremonies.

"Why have you brought us here?" Stein asked.

Drakos looked taken aback by the question. "To wait for the gold to be loaded, of course."

"The *Grigoro Fidi* is fast, but it was never designed to haul cargo." Stein was thinking out loud. "The *Medusa* is well hidden. The cave is perfectly camouflaged. Why not take the gold away on a more appropriate vessel? A cargo ship you can load under cover of night? One equipped with cargo booms and holds? It will take hours to load *Grigoro Fidi*."

Drakos said nothing. Toyed with his USP. The remainder of his bodyguards filed into the *katholikón*. Two stood on either side of the high altar. Others spread out around the ambulatory.

Hecate looked sharply at Stein. She'd underestimated the American. Looked at her as a woman, not a professional. Stein was observant. Considered exactly the same issues Hecate had considered.

"You wanted to bring us here this afternoon," Stein said, "in the *Grigoro Fidi*. You wanted to load the gold onto the yacht, but you wanted us all with you. Why?"

"Why do you think?"

"Breed's found this place." The triumph in Stein's voice was unmistakable. "He knows where you've hidden the *Medusa*. That's why you rushed us here in the *Fidi*. You were planning to transfer the gold to a freighter—a month from now. Breed's forced your hand."

"Yes," Drakos said. "He has. I expect he tried to call you, on the yacht. I've left a nasty surprise for him on Ésperos. Unfortunately, even if my men kill him, he must have made a report to authorities. They will come for us."

Hecate's heart pounded in her chest. Stein looked grim. "That's why you brought us."

"Of course," Drakos said, "I need hostages."

EVERY MOVEMENT CAUSES my stiff muscles to scream in pain. I get up and pace. Move my left arm in circles to loosen my shoulder. The movement loosens me up. My eyes are dark adapted. The moonlight is beautiful.

I turn to Hecate.

"Drakos means to escape in the *Grigoro Fidi* and took you all hostage. Somehow, you managed to escape."

"Yes," Hecate says. "Night fell. I asked to use the toilet. It was on the other side of the iconostasis, at the end of the nave. Drakos sent a bodyguard with me, and he waited outside. I found a window I could crawl through. Landed in the courtyard, ran to the nearest building, and found an unlocked door. I heard them come after me, tried to hide."

"They shot down my helicopter and killed three of the crew. A US destroyer is going to come for us. They'll stop the *Grigoro Fidi*."

"They'll free my father and Stein."

"It's not that simple. Once they've stopped the *Fidi*, there will be a standoff. Drakos will have his hostages to play."

"What do we do?"

"Free the hostages."

19

THE FOURTH DAY – PREDAWN, KOITÍDA SOFIAS

"How do we rescue them?" Hecate asks.

"They're being held in the *katholikón*. Drakos had six bodyguards. I've just killed two, which leaves four. Drakos heard the gunshots. That's got him wondering."

"What do you mean?"

"The first man I killed didn't have his gun drawn. He was looking for you in the dark. The other man who chased you down the hall? He didn't draw his gun until he saw me step into the corridor. Drakos told them to bring you back unharmed."

"He would not want to anger my father."

"Drakos doesn't know I'm here. He doesn't know why his men were shooting. He's going to send more to find out what's going on."

"Do you think he'll send them all?"

"No. He'll send two. They all have phones. When he can't reach Miklos and Sarkis, he'll assume something's wrong.

He'll think you've taken a weapon from his men and used it on them."

"He might call more men from the cave."

"I don't think so. He won't want to divert men to find one girl, armed or not. I reckon he has one man on the north wall, one man with him in the *katholikón*, and two men free to search."

My shoulder is throbbing from the impact of the falling rock. I rotate my arm, flex the muscle to maintain mobility. "We have to take Drakos by surprise. How many entrances are there to the *katholikón*?"

"Two that I know about. The secret staircase and the door at the end of the nave."

"It doesn't make sense, does it?"

"What do you mean?"

"This place is a thousand years old. Crete doesn't enjoy holiday weather all the time. Isn't it odd that the monks didn't build a covered passage to the church?"

"It's a short walk."

"They joined the other three buildings." I sit next to Hecate. "At a minimum, there's a ground-level entrance somewhere around the sanctuary. All churches have that. But I think there's another underground passage leading into that church. That's what we have to find."

"How can you be sure?"

"I'm not. But these medieval monks loved their secrets. A secret cave, a secret passage to the cave. Why not a secret passage connecting their refectory to the church?"

"Where?"

"It has to be in the basement. In *this* building, because it's the oldest."

"Alright. What do you want to do?"

"The first thing is to peel off whoever Drakos sends after us. I'm going to lead them away from you, then come back."

Hecate grabs my arm. "Don't leave me."

"You're safer here. Don't worry, they'll be too busy worrying about me."

I STEP through the darkened corridors of the monastery. Drakos won't want to uncover the north approach, so he'll send two men. Where are they? If I were in their shoes, I'd start from the bottom and push toward the top floor. A quarry trapped on the top floor is as good as dead.

Drakos's men are probably sweeping the ground floor right now.

I descend the staircase and turn off the light on the ground floor landing. Push the door open and enter the corridor. Everything is quiet. I push open a door to my right and enter a large chamber. Windowless, because it is against the high stone wall facing the cliff. The chamber is empty.

Turn, go into the chamber across the corridor. This one is equally large, but is graced by wide windows at ground level that look onto the courtyard. The *katholikón* occupies two-thirds of the space. The cruciform architecture isn't clear from this angle. It looks more like a rectangular building with two domes. The transepts are shadowy protrusions, probably occupied by chapels.

The view of the *katholikón* convinces me even more that there is an underground passage to the church. Greece isn't all sunshine and light. Ferocious storms lash the Aegean and Mediterranean. Those tempests have filled these waters with shipwrecks for three thousand years.

The room has a different arrangement than the libraries on the top floors. This room looks more like a classroom. Long rows of wooden desks sit in the dark. Low cabinets pushed against the wall stand empty. There's no moonlight here, despite the windows. This is the shadow side of the building.

It's a scriptorium. Centuries ago, before the advent of the printing press, monks sat here and copied books by hand. Most of those hand-copied books probably sit in the libraries of Koitída Sofías, Metéora, and Mount Athos.

I walk to the door and step back into the corridor. Look left, advance with the Mark 23 at retracted high ready.

A shadowy figure steps out of a room at the far end of the corridor. Shouts in Greek, opens fire with an MP5. Short burst, ten or fifteen rounds, half his magazine. Muzzle flashes flare like lightning in the dark space. I throw myself against the wall, extend the Mark 23, send two rounds down-range. The gunman dodges back into the room. Squeezes off a second burst.

I throw myself against the door that opens to the stair-well. A second man enters the corridor from the opposite stairwell, dumps a magazine in my direction. I slam the door shut behind me. Flinch as 9mm rounds splinter it into matchwood.

Pounding footsteps. The men are on their way, confident of their superior firepower. I run up the stairs to the first story, flick off the lights. I hear the ground floor door crash open, and I run to the second story. Flick off the lights there.

I'm leading the gunmen away from Hecate. They know I have NODs, they know that turning off the lights gives me an advantage. If I've turned off the lights on the first and second stories, I'm not on the first. They pound past the first story and start up the stairs to the second.

Leaning around a switchback, I send a couple of rounds downrange. Draw a hail of 9mm submachine gun fire. I turn and dash to the third story. Flick off the lights on the landing, run inside.

The lights are still off on the third story. Sarkis's body lies sprawled on the other end of the corridor. He'll keep these two busy for a while. They'll check to see if he's alive, they might look for Miklos. I dart back into the library I used to enter the monastery. Hurry onto the balcony and close the door behind me.

Holster the Mark 23. There are a couple of ways to do this, depending on what I want to achieve. If I want to go straight back down and rejoin Hecate, I can climb down the drainpipe to the first story, re-enter the building, and find her.

On the other hand, I can try to whittle down the enemy force. To do that, I want to get behind them. Achieve an element of surprise. This is not so easy.

I examine the windows. They run the length of the building. There are windows behind the balconies. There, they flank the balcony doors. The windows have thick wooden frames that protrude an inch and a half from the wall. Set around the frames are window casings, another half inch in thickness. The top of each casing is the head. The bottom of the casing is the stool, which is slightly thicker than the head. Beneath the stool is an ornamental apron, cut to look like the eaves that border the roof.

The structures all look sturdy enough. Standing close to the wall, I mount the balcony rail. It's wide enough to stand on. I place one hand against the wall for support, reach up to the eaves with the other. For a second, I stare at the dizzying drop.

I hear the door to the library open. Step onto the stool of the window to my left, test it with my weight. I grip the eaves with both hands. I can feel the wood of the eaves under my second knuckle. My fingertips are pressed against the galvanized iron of the gutter behind. I use the three points of contact to take my weight and shift my right foot to the stool.

Standing in this way, my stance is secure. I shift sideways past the first window and plant my left foot on the stool of the adjacent second window. Slide my hands along the eaves so I am braced between the first window and the second. Left foot on the stool of the second, right foot on the stool of the first, both hands on the eaves. Now I'm not facing a window. I'm facing the wall *between* the windows.

Take a breath, look down into the four-hundred-foot abyss. High winds could make things more interesting, but the air remains still. I'm perfectly safe. I could do this exercise five feet off the ground and not think twice.

In the dark, the pirates will see an empty library. If they look toward the windows, they will see nothing. Not even the toes of my shoes. If one of them should open the balcony door and stick his head out, it's his tough luck. I'll reach down with my right hand, draw the Mark 23, and blow his head off. I'll break a window and swing myself into the library before his buddy figures out what happened.

The pirates sweep through the library. I hear them blundering into furniture. Why don't they turn the lights on? They *know* I have NODs.

Lights blaze from the windows. They must have heard me thinking.

Of course, lighting the interior improves my situation.

The lights destroy the pirates' night vision and makes it impossible for them to see what's going on outside. Okay, I'll wait for them to leave and make their way to the next room. Then I'll re-enter the library and come up behind them.

The pirates leave the room. First, they'll move to the one across the corridor, then they'll go to the one next door to this one. When I'm sure they're in that one, I'll go back inside.

I return to the balcony. No need to repeat my cat burglar act. I'll make my move when they turn the lights on.

Flip up my NODs. The lights go on next door and I step back into the library. Open the door, enter the hall with my pistol drawn.

A *third* pirate pushes open the door to the opposite stairwell.

Shit.

Before the third man enters the corridor, I dodge back inside the library. Close the door. That makes it three-on-one. Had he seen me, things might have turned into a holy mess. I would have lost the element of surprise.

Plan B.

I walk to the balcony, close the door behind me, and mount the rail. Reach for the eaves with my left hand and the drain with my right. I keep an eye on the lighted windows. There's no sign I've been discovered. They'll clear this floor, then go downstairs to the second story.

Find a toehold against the wall with my right shoe. Release my grip on the eaves, transfer my left hand to the drain. Slowly, I make my way down. As I descend, I watch the lights in the third story windows go on one after another.

They're panicking. A few minutes ago, they were certain they could trap me on the third story. That's why they summoned the third man to join them from the opposite stairwell. Now they have no idea where I've gone.

I should have considered the possibility that Drakos would send help. It's a big monastery, and it's hard to find someone who doesn't want to be found. He's stripping his remaining force. This third man was either pulled off the north wall or sent from the sanctuary.

That Drakos is stripping his security force is a bad sign. It means he's focusing all his efforts on transferring the gold to *Grigoro Fidi*. He wants to leave before dawn.

The second story is dark, as is the first. I flip down my NODs. Find myself on the balcony outside the library where Hecate is hiding. This time, I know where the pirates are, so I don't worry too much about noise. Maybe I'm just exhausted and cranky because the arrival of the third man spoiled my ambush. I want to get into the *katholikón* and be done with this business.

I test the handle on the balcony door. Find it locked. Put my shoulder to it and hear the doorjamb groan. Draw back half an inch and shove hard. The wood splinters and the door bursts inward. I grab the doorknob with my right hand. Stop the door from slamming open.

Step into the darkness. The chamber looks empty, as it should. I bend at the waist, see an amorphous bundle crammed under the central reading table. It's Hecate, hiding. I walk over to her, crouch low, and offer my hand.

Hecate stares at my glowing green eyes with an expression of relief. She takes my hand and I help her up.

"They're on the top floor, but they'll be coming soon," I tell her. "We need to move fast."

I hold her hand and lead her into the corridor. We step into the darkened stairwell and descend to the basement.

The landing is lit. I switch off the light and examine the door.

There's no sign of light leaking from beneath the door. Gently, I release Hecate. Hold the Mark 23 in one hand, open the door with the other. I examine the interior through my NODs. There's a switch on the wall. I push my NODs up on my helmet and turn on the lights.

Together, Hecate and I step into the basement. I flick the light in the stairwell back on and shut the door behind us.

We're about to find out if I'm right. Did the monks build a passage to the *katholikón*?

20

THE FOURTH DAY – DAWN, BIE EIRINI

We find ourselves in a large, roomy basement with stone walls and a wooden ceiling. The wall to my right is definitely stone and mortar, twelve feet high. It must be a downward extension of the ground floor wall that I climbed to get into the monastery. This basement has been hewn from limestone, beneath the medieval scriptorium.

Regularly spaced wooden pillars support the ceiling above. The rafters are a maze. It's like the original builders designed the ceiling and pillars to form an integrated support system. Builders that followed over the years augmented that support system with cross-braces.

"The monks were afraid of cave-ins," Hecate says. "Earthquakes are a common occurrence in Greece."

I'm at a loss. Not sure what this basement was used for. It's devoid of furniture and decoration. There is a heavy door set in the opposite stone wall. I walk over to it with a measured step. The floor consists of wide, flat hexagonal stones. They've been fitted together in a clean pattern, joined with mortar.

The basement is dusty. There are cobwebs in the rafters. The monastery above is well maintained. The care and attention doesn't extend to the basement. Drakos apparently has no use for it.

I press the flat of my hand against the door. The wood is old and cracked. Iron hinges, painted black, show traces of rust where the paint has scraped away. I don't know how many times they have been replaced over the centuries. There's no lock on the door. I motion for Hecate to stand back, pull on the ironwork handle. The door opens with a metallic creak.

We step into a massive hall, a hundred and fifty feet long and thirty feet wide. The wooden pillars that support the vestibule ceiling continue the length of this chamber. They extend in two orderly rows all the way to a wooden door at the other end. The basement has been designed around this hall.

Long tables in the center of the chamber stretch the length of the room. The tables are bare, but straight-backed wooden chairs have been arranged along both sides. The hall is brilliantly lit by equally-spaced chandeliers. The tables are covered with tan dustcovers.

The difference between this hall and the vestibule is that here the walls are paneled with fine, polished wood. Decorated with religious mosaics and icons in colorful rows. There is a huge tapestry hung, floor to ceiling, in the center of the left wall. A tapestry of Christ, flanked on either side by armies of angels and demons. The edges of the tapestry are trimmed with golden tassels. Angels march on the left, demons march on the right. The two armies of good and evil are going to meet and do battle in the center.

To the right of the tapestry is a magnificent icon of the Archangel Michael. To the left is an icon of the Archangel Gabriel.

The hall looks like it has not been used in years.

"What is this place?" I ask.

"It looks like a refectory," Hecate says. "I have no idea why it would be located down here. I'm sure there will be another refectory in one of the buildings upstairs. This must have been intended for special occasions."

I stride the length of the room. Cautiously open the door on the other side, confirm it is a vestibule like the one through which we entered.

We have to find the secret passage. If it exists. Otherwise, we could end up facing three men with submachine guns. We've stayed ahead of them so far, but there's a good chance they'll break in on us from two sides. They could catch us in a crossfire. The only thing to do is go through one of these doors, charge into one group, and take them in a meeting engagement. At close quarters, my Mark 23 would be a match for an MP5.

"The passage has to be here," I say. "In *this* room. Look at the building. Four stories of libraries. Priceless books and art. This hall was built by the monks as a refectory. For group meals, prayer, and discussion. When they finished their business, they would go to the church."

Hecate walks to the end of the hall, comes back. The girl's attention is focused on the tapestry. "Do you think this is too obvious?"

"After reading *The Purloined Letter*, no place is too obvious."

The tapestry hangs from a black iron rod fixed an inch below the ceiling. The material is held flat by the weight of an identical iron rod to which its bottom edge has been attached. Hecate steps to one side of the tapestry and peeps behind it.

I glance left and right, strain my ears for the sound of pirates entering the vestibules.

"Look," Hecate says, "the tapestry's hiding something."

Sure enough, the two metal rods are hinged. They break in the middle and swing out as one. In fact, they are the top and bottom cross-pieces of an iron frame, hinged in the center. Hecate folds the tapestry in half, swings the frame open.

Behind the tapestry is the opening to a tunnel. It's a black maw, large enough for a man to enter upright.

"Here's your secret passage," Hecate says.

The door to my left opens, and two pirates enter, MP5s raised to their shoulders. I raise the Mark 23 and fire twice. The first round hits the Number One man in the weapon and ricochets into his throat. The second round hits him high in the chest. The man pitches backwards against his Number Two. His trigger finger clamps down reflexively and the MP5 discharges high into the wall. The burst splinters some beautiful paneling, chews up a couple of icons.

I sense movement behind me. Hecate dives into the tunnel. I throw myself prone on the stone floor. Feet spread apart, weapon extended in both hands. Number Two shoves his dying buddy out of the way in time to walk into my second double-tap. One round hits him in the middle of the chest. He has the MP5 pointed in my general direction and fires one-handed at where I used to be. Full auto, high rate of fire, the bullets scatter over my head as my second round hits him two inches above the first. He lands on his back, and the MP5 skids across the stone floor.

Get up, advance on the two pirates. Number Two is dead, his sightless eyes fixed on the ceiling. Number One is still alive, choking. Blood bubbles from the wound in his throat. The chest wound is high. Missed his heart, nicked the aorta. His MP5's receiver is hopelessly dented from my .45 round. No good to me. I take his spare magazines.

I pick up Number Two's MP5. From his hip pocket, I pluck two spare magazines. I straighten, put a bullet into Number One's face. Decock the Mark 23 and holster it. Sling the MP5 and walk back to Hecate.

"Did you have to kill him?"

"We're about to protect our rear. Come on."

I take Hecate by the elbow and lead her into the tunnel. Flip down my NODs and look as far as I can in the dark. The tunnel looks clear. I flip up the NODs, turn, and face the iron frame on which the tapestry has been mounted. Grasp the frame on the left and pull it shut. The tapestry blocks out the light from the room and we're left in darkness.

"Stay back," I tell Hecate.

I rack the bolt, pull the MP5's empty magazine, and drop it. Slide in one of the spares and charge the weapon. The MP5 is a beautiful weapon to shoot. For practical purposes, I like to use it as a semi-automatic carbine. On full auto, I restrict myself to two or three round bursts. I don't know anybody who hits anything by dumping a mag on full auto. On top of that, its rate of fire is so high, you can empty a mag in seconds.

Today, I'll make an exception. I leave the weapon on full auto and stand in the dark behind the tapestry. Gently push Hecate against the wall. "Be still."

I wait for the inevitable sound of the door on the left opening. The third pirate enters the hall. I imagine his reaction. Sees his friends dead on the floor, right next to the other door. He steps forward, conscious that Number Two's MP5 is missing. Concludes whoever killed the man has left through the opposite door.

He's cautious. I close my eyes, listen for his approach. The gentle scuff of rubber soles on the dusty stone floor. It's a zen-like experience for me, like point-shooting blindfolded. Toda Seigen, a sixteenth-century Japanese swordsman, knew he was losing his sight. He trained himself to fight blind.

The man comes closer. When I sense he's next to the tapestry, I squeeze the trigger, move the muzzle of the weapon in a tight little circle. The MP5 sounds like a buzz saw as bullets rip through the tapestry. I hear a grunt from the other side of the tapestry and a crash as the man falls against the wooden chairs. The MP5 clicks empty.

MP5s are nice. Firing from the closed bolt, you don't get that distracting *thunk* when a three-pound bolt slams on an empty chamber. The problem with open-bolt submachine guns is, you need that heavy bolt to retard their otherwise high rate of fire.

I drop the MP5 on its sling, push it behind me. Draw the Mark 23 and swing the frame open. Step into the hall with pistol extended. The pirate is on the floor next to a table, lying between two chairs. The MP5 mag packs thirty rounds. I fired chest high, hit him five or six times. Hit him in the arm, neck and chest. He's on the floor, bleeding out. His hand is still on his weapon, but he's not making an effort to bring it to bear.

Step forward, shoot him in the ear. His head cracks

against the floor. I separate him from his weapons system. Decock the Mark 23 and holster it. Relieve the man of his spare magazines. Rack the bolt, pull the mag from my MP5, reload. Go back in the tunnel, close the frame behind me.

Narrow beams of light stream through bullet holes in the tapestry. They play on Hecate's face and the walls of the tunnel. Not enough to light up the dark, but enough to remind us there's a world outside.

There aren't many pirates left. I know I've killed five, and I'll bet Drakos has kept one man with him. The tunnel is dark. I flip the NODs down.

"We're going to follow this tunnel," I say. "I can see with these, so hang on to me and stay close."

I think about the distance from the building to the *katholikón*. Estimate the length of the tunnel. If the tunnel runs straight and true, it should be sixty yards long. Of course, there's no requirement that it run straight and true.

We advance slowly through the tunnel, guided by the green glow of the NODs. I listen for sounds of pursuit. There are none.

The tunnel's walls and floor consist of smooth stone and mortar. The ceiling is shored up with heavy timber. Thirty feet along the tunnel, I stop. Blink in the night vision, not sure what I'm looking at is real.

Something's different about the walls. They're still stone and mortar, but they're recessed on both sides. Alcoves have been cut into the stone. Each is rectangular in shape, ten feet wide and four feet deep. There's a stone shelf at the back, about a foot high and a foot deep.

My stomach clenches. Arranged along the shelves, on both sides of the tunnel, are rows of skulls. Clean and white, staring at me through gaping holes where eyes used to be.

Beneath each skull, sitting on the floor in the alcove, is a stone box. The forehead of each skull bears a number. A few of the skulls have names written on them in black marker.

"Oh God."

"What is it?" Hecate whispers.

"This tunnel is an ossuary. I think it holds the remains of every monk who's ever passed away at Koitída Sofias."

"That makes sense," Hecate says. "It's an orthodox tradition. The monks would keep the bones in a private place, away from the public eye. There may be more than one tunnel like this. Other monasteries keep ossuaries above ground in designated chambers."

"Doesn't it creep you out?"

"Of course not. It's life... and death, which is the same thing. I visited the Great Metéoron monastery in Thessaly. They have an above-ground ossuary where they display the skulls of the founding monks."

How wise. Hecate's right, but the hairs are standing up on the back of my neck. I try to keep my mind focused on the task at hand. For all her brave words, Hecate clutches me more tightly. She's not following me along the tunnel anymore—we're walking side by side. I'm the big, strong guy with the submachine gun, but the warmth of this woman holding onto me makes me feel better.

The tunnel ends in a chamber twelve feet square. My NODs reveal bare stone walls and a heavily timbered roof. There's a table shoved against one wall. There are rusted metal tools on the table. They look like they haven't been used since the last time Koitída Sofias was a working monastery.

"There's a table and metal tools," I tell Hecate. "I think we're under the *katholikón*."

"It's part of the ossuary," Hecate says. "Bodies were buried for two years. When the process of natural decomposition was complete, they were exhumed, blessed, and the bones cleaned before final internment. This had to be a respectful, holy process."

A wooden staircase leads upward. At the top of the steps is a black square—a trapdoor.

Hecate's grip tightens around my arm. Gently, I pry her fingers loose. Hold them tight, whisper in her ear. "I'm going up the steps. Wait until I signal, be quiet when you follow me."

I release Hecate's fingers and climb the steps. When I reach the trapdoor, I stop and listen. The sound of voices carries from the other side. Muffled, as though coming from a great distance.

In the center of the wooden square is an iron handle. I grip it, push against the bottom of the trapdoor, and swing it open an inch. Find myself peering into a small, dark room. On the other side of the room, my NODs reveal a wooden panel. There's a sliver of light at the bottom.

I keep a firm grip and push the trapdoor wide. It's an inch thick and heavier than I thought. It won't do to have it crash open. I climb into the room and examine the trapdoor's top surface. A handle and a metal notch have both been screwed into the wood. I see a hinged metal rod, two feet long, lying on the floor. It's been designed to fit into the notch to prop up the heavy slab. I engage the rod and tug the handle on the bottom surface. The trapdoor is secure.

Hecate is looking up at me. I reach down, take her hand, and help her up the steps. I assume this dark room is a vestibule to conceal the *katholikón's* end of the tunnel. There must be a light, but I haven't found the switch.

I turn back to the panel separating us from the lighted room. Flip up my NODs and push gently. The panel gives way and reveals a beautiful chamber. The walls are paneled with fine wood, decorated with icons. Tables within are covered with rich cloth. More icons grace the tabletops. Set on one of the tables are a golden candelabra and tabernacle. The latter is a gleaming domed vessel reserved for the consecrated Eucharist.

The chamber's empty. It can't be the sacristy—that chamber lies above the stone steps that lead to the cave. No, this must be the vestry, on the opposite side of the high altar. Ten feet away is a wooden door. That must lead into the sanctuary. The voices are coming from the other side.

I step to the vestry door and open it a crack.

The high altar is a thing of beauty. Surrounded by icons, covered with gilded and tasseled cloth. Tapered candles sit in golden candelabra. Stained glass windows stand dark against the night sky. A grand dome, displaying an icon of Christ, graces the ceiling. The dome is discreetly illuminated by concealed lights.

A rail of polished red wood circles the sanctuary. Three short staircases of three steps each lead from the ambulatory to the dais. There are gaps in the rail where the steps are. The rail has been placed to prevent accidental falls.

The altar faces the iconostasis. Within the sanctuary, between the altar and the wall of icons, are two sets of beautifully carved, high-backed wooden chairs. What did Hecate call them? Stacidia. Facing me, Drakos sits on one of the chairs. He holds a USP Compact in his right hand, pointed at Stein, Harding-James, and Kyrios.

One of Drakos's bodyguards is standing at the high altar. He wears a USP at his hip. Slung over his shoulder is an

MP5. On the way here, I killed two bodyguards on the top floor, and three in the basement. That makes five. I think this guy is the last of Drakos's personal security detail. He's been pulled off the north approach.

That means Drakos is no longer concerned about security in the monastery. He must be ready to leave.

I doubt Drakos heard the most recent exchange of gunfire. The shootout occurred in the basement. The stone walls and earth probably muffled the shots.

Drakos has the pistol in his right hand and a mobile phone in the left. He's trying to contact his men and coming up empty.

What's he going to do now? Call for reinforcements? Move the hostages to the *Grigoro Fidi*? It won't be long before he makes a move. The pirates in the cave are almost finished transferring the gold. Drakos will move everyone to the cave.

Dawn is coming, and with it, Lieutenant Morgan's SEALs.

Drakos snaps orders in Greek. Gestures with his USP. The bodyguard with the MP5 leads the way toward the sacristy. Stein, Harding-James, and Kyrios follow him. Drakos brings up the rear.

From the sacristy, they'll descend the staircase to the cave.

I have a decision to make.

Flick the selector switch on the MP5 to semi-automatic, step onto the ambulatory floor. I raise the weapon to my shoulder and fire twice. The bodyguard's head jerks, and he tumbles down three steps to the ambulatory.

Stein dives for the sanctuary floor. Harding-James and Kyrios whirl in the direction of the shots. Drakos grabs the nearest hostage—Kyrios—and steps behind him. Holds the USP to his head and uses him for cover.

"Put the weapon down, Breed."

MP5 to my shoulder, I step onto the sanctuary. Hold the weapon on Drakos, looking for the shot. He'll take the USP from Kyrios's head to shoot me, and I'll take him down. It'll happen in an instant.

"Do what he says, Breed."

I know that voice.

Harding-James is holding a Glock 42 on me. Lovely weapon. Modern sub-compact, six rounds .380 ACP, polymer-framed. The kind of pistol I'd buy my girlfriend or mom. The kind an English gentleman would carry. How did he get it? It's illegal to own in England, much less carry.

They've got me cold. Either man could shoot me dead. I lower the MP5.

"The pistol too," Drakos says. "Very slowly."

I set the Mark 23 on the floor.

Drakos relaxes. "Now, Hecate. Join us."

Hecate steps onto the sanctuary. "Let my father go."

"Of course." Drakos releases Kyrios. The old man steps back, outraged.

I look from Harding-James to Drakos. "You had to get the *Medusa*'s cargo and schedule somewhere. Who better than the lead underwriter?"

"Simple profit calculation, Breed." The Englishman looks pleased with himself. "I lose fifty million dollars insurance and receive six hundred million in gold. I'll do that business all day."

"Why did you bother to involve us?"

"There will be a determined investigation. I had to put on a convincing act, didn't I? Of course, I had to pull every string, try every avenue to find *Medusa*. That, and fifty million of my own money in the syndicate should be enough to convince anyone of my innocence. Skin in the game, old chap. Does wonders for a man's credibility."

"That's enough," Drakos says. "Breed, the only reason you're still alive is—I want what *you* know."

"How trite."

"Perhaps. But you never completed your call to Stein. Who else knows the *Medusa* is in Bie Eirini?"

"I should think that's obvious."

"Humor me."

"The United States Navy. The Hellenic Navy. Everybody."

"What are they up to?"

"They are going to arrest you, of course. Or kill you. I doubt they care which. I have to say, one of the worst things about the European Union is its abolition of the death penalty."

Harding-James sniffs. "There is no death penalty anywhere for hijacking."

"I'm not talking about hijacking. I'm talking about murder."

The Englishman looks genuinely shocked. "Murder?"

"You didn't know? Drakos had the crew of the *Medusa* murdered. They're all eighteen fathoms under Bie Eirini, entombed in Hold Number Two."

"No, no, no!" Kyrios shakes his head and recoils. "You put them off on an island."

"Why would I take a chance on their early rescue?"

"It was *agreed*. There would be no unnecessary killing."

Hecate stares at her father with wide eyes. "Father, were you involved?"

The girl's shock is as convincing as her father's. The old man is shaking from Drakos's admission. He's unable to speak.

Harding-James laughs. "Dear Hecate, of course he was. What do you buy a man who has everything? A thrill. Thanos saw this little adventure as a delightful game."

"Enough." With a sharp tone, Drakos cuts off the Englishman. "Breed, who is coming? When, and how?"

"I don't know, Drakos. I'm afraid that's up to them. Little Indians like me don't get to decide shit."

"Then they won't mind if I kill one little Indian." Drakos raises his USP and levels it at my chest.

Kyrios clubs Drakos's arm with his fist. There's a shot, incredibly loud in the closed space of the sanctuary. The bullet skids off the floor.

Harding-James cries out, clutches his groin. The Glock 42 rattles on the stone.

I hurl myself at Drakos. The burly Greek grabs Kyrios by the jacket, swings the old man between us and shoves him into me. For such a large man, Drakos is incredibly agile. He jumps down the sanctuary steps, hurdles his dead body-guard, and dodges into the sacristy.

Stein snatches the Glock 42 from the floor and covers Harding-James and Kyrios. The Englishman is curled into a ball, hands pressed to the inside of his left thigh. Blood soaks his pants leg and spreads in a puddle on the stones.

I grab the MP5 and Mark 23. Run after Drakos.

Submachine gun raised to my shoulder, I approach the sacristy door. I only have Hecate's description of the chamber to guide me. I step to one side of the door, push it open, and dig the right corner. Nothing. At the back of the room, a false wall stands ajar.

I'm not about to rush into the room and get clipped by Drakos firing from a blind spot. I step to the other side of the door, dig the left corner. The sacristy is empty.

I go to the varnished wooden panel at the back. No need for NODs in here. The stone staircase leading to the cave is lit by bulbs strung along the ceiling. The stairs twist counter-clockwise, designed to assist defenders who are retreating toward the cave.

Hecate told me there were over one thousand steps in this staircase. The twist is so sharp there is no way either of us is going to get off a shot. It's a question of reaching the bottom as quickly as possible. If Drakos gets there first, he'll turn around and shoot me as I come off the steps.

I'm not going to let that happen. I won't burst from the stairwell. I'll use the bend in the staircase for cover. If I catch him before he gets to the bottom, I'll kill him with my bare hands.

There's a thump and clatter below me. Drakos swears in Greek.

You can run *up* stairs two or three at a time. Dashing *down* stairs is tougher. You can't skip two or three, especially when the steps are narrow. If you fall down the stairs you can break a leg, break an arm.

Too much to hope for. Drakos's footsteps continue to skip down the staircase. These steps will *never* end.

Pop, pop, pop.

Bullets whine off the stone next to my face. Rock chips sting my cheek. I check my forward momentum, duck behind the curve of the staircase.

Most people will expect me to look around the curve at

eye level. They'll wait to blow my face off. On the street, I would drop prone to look around. Can't do that on a staircase, so I drop to a low crouch. Peer around the curve.

I take in the whole cave with one glance. Drakos has taken cover behind an electric crane on the dock. The crane is in the process of lifting a pallet of gold onto the stern of the *Grigoro Fidi*. Drakos is firing his USP at me. I squeeze off three rounds to return fire.

The *Grigoro Fidi*, all one hundred and twenty feet of her, lies tied up to the dock. Sixty pallets, two billion dollars. There are only three pallets left. Crew in white uniforms and other men in dark shirts and blue jeans have been working all night to transfer the cargo. Most of the men in dark shirts are carrying MP5s. The crew in white are carrying M4 carbines.

Spotlights mounted in the roof of the cavern illuminate the *Grigoro Fidi*. The gullet of the cave is brightly lit, but the recesses are cloaked in shadow. Beyond the bow of the *Fidi* is the camouflage screen that Hecate described. From where I crouch, it looks seamless, though the dawn is breaking on the other side.

The weapons make sense. The men in dark shirts are Drakos's men. The men in white are Kyrios's crew. Drakos's men carry German weapons, Kyrios's crew carry American weapons. It doesn't matter—they're on the same side.

I squeeze off three more rounds. The bullets strike sparks from the crane.

Drakos snaps orders in Greek. It's not hard to figure out what he's up to. There are two dozen men in the cave. They're either on the dock or on the yacht, and they're armed. If they rush me, I'm cooked. Three of the men around Drakos open fire with MP5s on full auto. Not accurate, but enough to pin me down. Another man runs forward.

I flip the MP5 to full auto and stick it around the corner. Fire without aiming, move the muzzle in a tight circle. I learned that in Afghanistan. American operators were trained to use accurate, aimed fire. The Talis had numbers on their side, and they often didn't aim. They'd stick their AKs over a rock and do mag dumps. If they filled a volume with enough lead, they were bound to hit something.

It works. I'm rewarded with a cry. My MP5 clicks empty and I jerk it back behind cover. One of the pirates is rolling on the dock. I rack the bolt, jerk the empty mag from the MP5 and drop it. Pull a spare mag from my hip pocket and seat it in the mag well. Charge the weapon. Good to go.

Drakos shouts more commands. There's a loud whine as the *Grigoro Fidi*'s four turbine power plants start up.

More bullets ricochet off the curve of the staircase. Fly past and splatter the stone behind me. I stick the MP5 around the curve and let fly a second time. I'm conscious of the MP5's high rate of ammunition expenditure. At eight hundred rounds a minute, a single magazine is only good for three bursts.

Loud whacks fill the air. Everyone in the cave looks toward the camouflage screen. It appears black from inside the cave, but four circular areas are lightening. Two on the left side of the screen, two on the right. Incendiaries have been fired at the screen from outside the cave.

The screen's on fire. First, the circular spots elongate upwards, then the original circles burn through. The canvas melts away and the fire spreads. In seconds, the cave mouth has been exposed.

Dawn has broken. The sky is lightening from east to

west. There are a few clouds on the horizon, tinged salmon pink.

Standing half a mile off Bie Eirini, the USS *Pressley Bannon* presents her port side to the cave mouth. Much closer, less than a hundred yards from the cave mouth, two Combat RIBS—Rubber Inflatable Boats—speed toward us. Their white bow waves trace inverted Us in the blue water. Lying flat in the boats are SEALs in combat camouflage uniforms. Five men to a boat. One man manages the outboard, four have suppressed M4s pointing over the prow of the RIB.

The SEALs open fire.

21

THE FOURTH DAY – MORNING, BIE EIRINI

Drakos dodges from behind the crane. Lunges toward the *Grigoro Fidi* and leaps for the fantail. I can't believe the big guy clears it. For a brief moment, he teeters on the edge of the rail. One of the crew leaps forward and extends his hand. Drakos grasps it and the crewman hauls him aboard.

More shouted commands. The crewman rushes to the stern line and casts off. Another crewman casts off from the bow.

The men who had been firing at me turn their weapons on the SEALs. Firing suppressed M4s, Morgan's men cut them down without mercy. Bullets stitch the pirates. When you're hit by an M4, you don't go flying back. You remain standing while the small, high-velocity bullets tumble inside you. They cause massive destruction. They shatter bones or punch grotesque wounds through soft tissue.

Drakos makes his way forward and disappears into the saloon. The water at the *Grigoro Fidi*'s stern boils as the four powerful screws spin up. The yacht pushes forward, cleaving the waters between the two RIBs. The SEALs leap from the boats as they are swamped in the *Grigoro Fidi*'s wake. Some land on the dock, others fall into the water and claw their way out.

Pirates take cover behind the cranes and two remaining pallets of gold. They fire at the SEALs floundering in the water.

Morgan's standing on the dock, helping his men. He has one SEAL by the arm. A pirate fires from behind a pallet of gold. The man Morgan is helping jerks as the bullet shatters his clavicle.

I fire a short, three-round burst. One bullet cracks a plastic case and squashes against a gold brick. The other two rounds hit the pirate in the face. He drops his weapon and reels backward. At the sound of firing, Morgan's head snaps in my direction. He recognizes me and we nod acknowledgment.

The SEALs fan out and engage the pirates on the docks. They don't stop, they attack and keep pushing. They're not there to take prisoners. These guys know their business. In the confines of the cave, their suppressors protect our ears.

Four SEALs didn't arrive on the RIBs. They're wearing wetsuits and Dräger LAR 8000 rebreathers. These must be the pathfinders who scouted the cave entrance last night. They determined that the camouflage screen was canvas and could be burned away. Remained hidden among the rocks and waited for the *Pressley Bannon* to arrive. Morgan and Palomas decided to attack straight up the middle.

One of the SEALs is carrying an M4 with an under-barrel M203 grenade launcher. He fires a grenade into one of the secondary chambers. There's a muffled explosion, followed by a whoosh. A crackling blowtorch of flame spurts from the chamber mouth. The *Grigoro Fidi*'s turbines run on MGO—marine gas oil—and the pirates must have stored fuel in that chamber.

Pirates at the chamber mouth are incinerated—black stick figures dance in the flames. The SEALs flatten themselves on the dock.

The other pirates take cover behind the cranes and sea sleighs. The SEALs get to their feet and keep pushing.

I sprint along the dock. The *Fidi*'s halfway out of the cave. I pump my arms like my life depends on it. I have to get onto the fantail. If I miss, those screws will grind me to hamburger.

No time to think, just act. I'm running out of dock. The *Grigoro Fidi*'s bow is already nosing out of the cave mouth. I take a running leap for the fantail. Take off from the dock, terrified my toe will slip on a slick plank. Feel blessed relief as my shoe finds a firm grip. Catapult myself through the air over the boiling wake and thrashing screws.

There's a jolt as I smash against the fantail. I clutch the rail for dear life. For a horrifying moment, my legs dangle over the screws. I'm face-to-face with the crewman on the after well deck. The man is carrying his M4 at port arms, too close to me to use it. He tries to back up to make room to shoot me. He should have short-stocked the weapon and blown my face off.

I grab the sling of the M4 with my right hand and haul. Pull him close, try to climb over him to get into the boat. The man tries to push me off. Left hand on mine, he tries to pry my fingers off the sling. Shoves his right hand in my face.

My left hand grabs the side of his head. Get my thumb into the corner of his right eye, next to his nose. Dig deep, use my thumb like a spoon. Scoop the eyeball out. He screams and lets go of the rifle. Grabs my left wrist with both hands. I hold his head like a bowling ball with my fingers grasping his ear and my thumb in his eye socket. Grab his shirt with my right hand and haul myself over the rail.

Spill onto the well deck. Left hand holding the man's head, right hand on his shirt. I punch him in the side, and his grip loosens. Grab his left leg, straighten at my knees, pitch him over the fantail.

With a scream, he falls into the *Grigoro Fidi*'s wake. Gets sucked into the screws like he's been dumped into a blender. For a second, the wake froths red and a fountain of chum is hurled into the air.

The yacht has opened up to maximum speed. It's raced past the USS *Pressley Bannon* and is heading for open sea. Already, Koitída Sofias and Bie Eirini are fading in the distance. I'm not sure what Drakos is doing, but he must have formulated a plan the moment he learned I found the *Medusa*. He's probably heading for Egypt or Libya.

There's a puff from the *Pressley Bannon*'s forward 5-inch gun mount. The shell sounds like a freight train rumbling overhead. There's an explosion and a geyser of water a hundred yards ahead of the yacht.

An electronically amplified voice belts over the water. "Attention, *Grigoro Fidi*. This is United States Navy warship. Stop and prepare to be boarded."

The *Grigoro Fidi* ignores the warning shot.

Commander Palomas has a number of ways of stopping the *Grigoro Fidi*. I want to make sure her final choice does not involve Breed getting blown to kingdom come.

Pallets have been arranged like tiles across the yacht's well deck. The yacht wasn't designed to transport thirty tons of gold, so they wanted to spread the weight as evenly as possible. They've done a good job. Pallets cover the well deck on both sides from the fantail to the saloon, with clear corridors in the middle and at the gunwales to allow people to pass.

The *Pressley Bannon* launches its Sea Hawk. I had this conversation with Kyrios two nights ago. The *Fidi* might outrun a warship, but it can't outrun a helo. The Sea Hawk closes on us from astern.

Stop and prepare to be boarded!

Two crewmen are standing on the navigation bridge. One of them shoulders a long, olive drab tube. I recognize the IFF antennae and battery coolant unit. A Stinger! He points it at the helicopter, trying for an infrared lock. Palomas knows the pirates are armed with Stingers. She would have warned the pilots to tune their infrared countermeasures to the peculiarities of the Stinger's sensor.

I raise the MP5 to my shoulder. Flick the weapon to semiautomatic, aim and fire. The man carrying the tube jerks, a crimson flower blooming on his chest. He drops the tube and falls from view.

The sharp crack of an M4 splits the air. In the dim interior of the saloon, I spot a muzzle flash. A crewman is firing at me. This man has set his M4 on semi-automatic. Seems to know what he's doing, but the pitching of the *Grigoro Fidi*'s deck caused him to miss.

The Stinger team is less of a threat, so I run to the side of the well deck. Look for cover, duck behind a pallet piled with plastic cases of gold. The MP5's 9mm NATO ball is a small, low-powered round. The M4 fires a high velocity 5.56mm. I'm not convinced the ship's bulkheads will stop bullets, but gold bricks will.

I scurry along the port gunwale and dive behind a bulkhead at the entrance to the saloon. Flatten myself against the deck. The man fires through the wall above me, about chest-high. I draw the Mark 23 from my holster. Peer around the corner into the saloon, catch him looking the wrong way.

Raise the pistol, fire twice. Both rounds go into his belly. The man grunts, goes down. I scramble to my feet, brace myself against the saloon door, shoot him in the head.

The Sea Hawk is orbiting the *Grigoro Fidi*. I decock the Mark 23, holster it, and go back outside. The second man in the Stinger team has shouldered the missile. There's a brief flash from the rocket's backblast and a whoosh as the rocket leaves the tube. The helo pilot takes evasive action. Shoves the collective, stamps on the right pedal, and the Sea King plunges toward the waves.

I brace myself against a funnel. The four turbine power plants are at maximum output and I feel the deck throbbing under my feet. I raise the MP5 to my shoulder. The man struggles to raise a second Stinger. I fire twice and he crumples like he's been cut in half.

The Sea Hawk has dropped to a hundred and fifty feet. The pilot hauls on the collective and adds power. The rotors claw the air and the helo roars around the *Fidi*. The Stinger has disappeared into the distance. The missile's IR sensor never properly locked the helo.

Step into the saloon. Take in the bar, tables, and plush leather seats. Was it only two nights ago Kyrios entertained us in this room? The weapons panel has been opened, the armory looted for rifles and Stingers. A crewman steps from the bridge, raising an M4. Before he can bring the weapon to his shoulder, I fire. One round enters his left cheek and blows half his face away. He falls sideways, discharging his weapon into the bulkhead. My second round misses and spends itself on the bridge windows. The man sprawls on the deck and I fire a third round into the pulp exposed beneath his cracked skull.

I look back through the saloon toward the fantail. The Sea Hawk has orbited the *Grigoro Fidi*. From astern, the helo's door gun unleashes a stream of tracers. It's a General Electric M134 Gatling gun. Rotary barrels, belt-fed, electrically driven, .308 caliber. It lays down six thousand rounds a minute. That's one hundred rounds a second. It sounds like a buzz-saw. Whether you are flying a jet fighter at five hundred miles an hour or a helo at a hundred and fifty, you get very short engagement windows. You want to send as many rounds downrange as you can in the second or two the target is in your sights.

Minigun fire rips into the yacht's fantail, props and rudders.

The *Fidi* lurches hard to port. I'm thrown from my feet and pitch hard against the sofa. Get up and struggle toward the bridge. Rudders jammed and propellers damaged, the *Fidi* slows down and powers forward in a wide circular track.

I raise the MP5 to my shoulder. Kick the dead crewman's rifle aside, step over his body, enter the bridge. Three men in the wheelhouse. Drakos, the captain, and the helmsman. The helmsman is sitting in his pilot's seat, struggling with controls that refuse to answer.

Drakos turns on me, USP raised. At a range of less than ten feet, we fire simultaneously. His round goes into the bulkhead behind my right ear. My first round drills him in the mouth. His head snaps back and the second round goes into his nose. He drops where he stands.

I turn the MP5 on the captain. The man raises his hands.

"Kill the power," I tell him.

The man's frozen. Either he doesn't understand English, or he's in shock. Maritime officers are supposed to have a *minimal* level of English. I remember Kyrios telling me his captain was once a Kriegsmarine officer. "*Halte das boot!*"

I step to the right side of the bridge, lean against the tilted deck. Don't want to be ambushed by anyone coming up from the accommodation deck. I hold the MP5 on the captain and helmsman, keep one eye on the companionway from above.

The Sea Hawk shadows the *Fidi*, takes up station off the yacht's starboard bow. It's no mean feat with the yacht racing in a circle. They're so close I can see the door gunner staring at us over his minigun's barrel cluster. Palomas is close to ordering them to take out the bridge crew. Firing six thousand rounds a minute, that weapon will rip this bridge apart in seconds.

"*Halte das boot! Schnell!*"

The helmsman chops the throttles. *Grigoro Fidi* slows to a stop and rolls gently in the waves. The Sea Hawk hovers twenty yards off the bow, its minigun pointed at us.

I step forward and kick Drakos's USP aside. Stare at the pirate and the spreading puddle of blood beneath his head.

The USS *Pressley Bannon* catches up to the yacht. Palomas stands off three hundred yards, lowers a whaleboat and an armed boarding party.

I lean back against the bulkhead and allow myself to breathe.

THE STAIRCASE from the cave to Koitída Sofias hasn't gotten any shorter. I lead Commander Palomas and eight sailors to the monastery. Palomas is wearing a sidearm, a SIG M17 on a web belt. Six of the sailors wear body armor and carry M4 carbines. Bringing up the rear are the *Pressley Bannon*'s doctor and a corpsman.

Morgan's SEALs are mopping up the cave complex. The wounded are being triaged by corpsmen, and serious cases are ferried to the *Pressley Bannon* in the whaleboat. The dead have been arranged in rows on the dock. Burned corpses carried from the fuel storage chamber have been covered with whatever material was at hand.

I step into the sacristy and push open the door that leads to the sanctuary. Stein and Hecate are sitting together on stacidia. Harding-James is lying on the stone floor. He's at the center of a crimson lake.

Stein's hands are brown with dried blood. "Took you long enough, Breed."

"Where's Kyrios?"

"He got away while I was trying to save Harding-James."

The *Pressley Bannon*'s doctor examines the Englishman. "He's dead. The shot clipped the femoral artery."

"Which way did Kyrios go?" Palomas asks Stein.

"I didn't see. When I stood up and looked around, he was gone."

Palomas turns to Hecate. "What about you? What did you see?"

"I was also focused on Ash."

Palomas draws a squad radio from a holster on her pistol belt. Walks to the iconostasis and keys the device.

"Where's Drakos?" Stein asks.

"He didn't make it." I study Harding-James's corpse. "I guess Kyrios saved my life."

"Yes. I wonder if he really did get involved for fun."

"We have all the pieces now. Harding-James saw the opportunity, and he brought the idea to Kyrios. The old man was close to retirement. He figured it would be an entertaining adventure to go out on. So long as no one got hurt."

Hecate joins us, arms folded. "My father would never agree to murdering innocent people."

I like her use of the word *innocent*. Her father knew Drakos's men executed her kidnapper.

"Kyrios brought Drakos into the picture," Stein says. "He knew Drakos would be happy to provide muscle."

"But Drakos was impossible to control." I look at Hecate. "Thinking back, Drakos was the captain of the *Goliath*. He was the one who ordered the crew to use hand grenades on me. He and his men chased me to the hotel. The following day, you drove us to Ésperos. Drakos had his men set up an ambush. They planned to stop us on the road, haul me and Stein out of the car and shoot us."

"That's why you thought it was a kidnap attempt," Stein tells Hecate. "In the first instance, they didn't want to kill you and Harding-James. They set up the roadblock to look like a stalled car."

"I don't think your father knew about the attempt until afterward," I say. "Already, he was losing control of Drakos. For your father, the heist was a game. For Drakos, it was much more. When I found *Medusa*, the stakes for Drakos were raised again. Your father was happy to walk away. Drakos couldn't let it go."

"Do you think Kyrios bought into Drakos taking the *Grigoro Fidi*?" Stein asks.

"He wasn't happy about it, but he had to. He obviously gave Drakos operational control of the *Grigoro Fidi* and its crew. I reckon when Drakos got word that I had found

Medusa, he called a council of war. Met with Kyrios and Harding-James. His plan was to load the gold onto the *Fidi* and run to North Africa. Kyrios and Harding-James would play hostage to help Drakos get away, and they could carve up the loot afterward. That's why Drakos held the gun on all of you. At every stage, he gave Kyrios and Harding-James plausible deniability. When I cornered him, the game was up, and Harding-James broke cover."

Commander Palomas rejoins us at the high altar. "Kyrios won't get far. We've alerted the Hellenic authorities and they'll lock this island tight."

Hecate meets my eyes.

"Ms Kyrios," Palomas says, "the authorities will want to speak with you. I understand you are an executive of Kyrios Shipping."

"Of course," Hecate says. "I run the local Greek operations. I assure you, I knew nothing of this."

I turn to Palomas. "Commander, I can vouch for her. Not long ago, Drakos's men were making every effort to kill us both. She was as surprised as anyone by this set-up."

"The Hellenic authorities will take your statements in Heraklio. We'll fly you there, sort everything out."

THE SEA HAWK puts down on a small flat patch outside Koitída Sofias's north gate. The helo sits with its rotor turning lazily while the pilots wait for us to board. The sun is warm and bright. I'm physically exhausted, but free from tension. I feel like all the questions that matter have been answered.

Stein takes me by the arm and draws me aside.

"Breed, I'm sorry for yesterday morning."

The thought of her and Kyrios had been eating me all that night, and much of yesterday. When I wasn't doing things like diving on sunken bullion ships and scaling four-hundred-foot cliffs. Less than sixty hours have passed since I first boarded the *Goliath* in Port Cymos.

"I'm sorry too. I overreacted."

"Let's forget it, okay?" She touches my arm.

"Do you think Greece does this to everybody?" I ask.

"I don't know. The islands, the sun..."

Before she can finish, I lean in and give Stein a hug. She hugs me back, and we hold each other for a minute.

Hecate clears her throat. Stein and I let go and turn to face her.

"I think we should be going," Hecate says.

We board the Sea Hawk, and the flight engineer hands us helmets with intercom headsets. Shows us where to sit, how to buckle into the H-frame gunner's seats. Stein and I sit together on the starboard side, facing outboard. Hecate and a door gunner sit behind us, facing in the opposite direction. This Sea Hawk has been configured for marine interdiction and sports two miniguns.

The flight engineer lowers himself into his jump seat and gives the pilot a thumbs-up. The twin engines spin up, and it becomes impossible to carry on a conversation without resorting to the intercom. I look toward the monastery and see Commander Palomas standing by the north gate.

The Sea Hawk speeds north toward Heraklio. It's midday, and the view of the Dikti mountains and Mount Spathi is dazzling.

Stein and I sit together in a comfortable silence. Her thoughts are a million miles away. Did she let Harding-

James die so Kyrios could escape? I don't think so. A severed femoral artery is a death sentence. Stein tried her best to save Harding-James. That said, she and Hecate *must* have seen Kyrios leave.

The three of us share a secret. We'll stick to our story, and no one will get us to say different. No one in Greece is going to give the Deputy Director of the CIA the third degree. No one's going to challenge the Executive Vice President of Kyrios Shipping, the owner of football clubs who can put thousands of protestors on the street with a phone call.

The gold will be returned to its owners, and Lloyd's will keep its money.

A cover story will be devised. The *Medusa* will have been lost in a tragic accident. The crew's next of kin will receive substantial insurance payouts. The *Medusa*, as a marine casualty, won't make the front page. It will be gone from the news in a day.

Below us, I see a speck. An old man, dressed like a mountain peasant, is picking his way over a goat trail. He looks up at our helo, doffs his cap, and waves. I swear he's laughing. Hecate told me her father had wealth hidden in a hundred countries, a hundred escape routes.

Athanasios Kyrios will never be found.

THE END
TO TEΛOΣ

ACKNOWLEDGMENTS

This novel would not have been possible without the support, encouragement, and guidance of my agent, Ivan Mulcahy, of MMB Creative. I would also like to thank my publishers, Brian Lynch and Garret Ryan of Inkubator Books for seeing the novel's potential. Thanks go to Claire Milto of Inkubator Books for her support in the novel's launch.

The novel benefitted from the feedback of my writing group and Beta readers. Conversations with my friends from Greece were particularly valuable. They provided insight into that country's music and traditions. Greek mythology, not at all distant, illuminates the natures of modern Greeks and their interactions. I learned much in writing this novel, and for that I am grateful.

If you could spend a moment to write an honest review, no matter how short, I would be extremely grateful. They really do help readers discover my books.

Feel free to contact me at cameron.curtis545@gmail.com. I'd love to hear from you.

ALSO BY CAMERON CURTIS

Made in United States
Orlando, FL
04 December 2024

54969555R00152